MYSTERY
ON THE
MOSELLE

RIVER CRUISE
COZIES
BOOK THREE

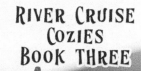

CHERYL DOUGAN

MYSTERY ON THE MOSELLE

A RIVER CRUISING COZY MYSTERY

CHERYL DOUGAN

DOUGAN PRESS

DOUGAN PRESS

Read a sample of the first chapter of the next book for free!
All you have to do is visit this link, https://tinyurl.com/cheryldougan4, enter your email address, and the free chapter will be on its way to you!

Interior Design by STOKE Publishing.

CONTENTS

CHAPTER 1
TRIER, GERMANY
HOME AWAY FROM HOME

Adelle tingled with excitement as she entered the ship's restaurant. She had dreamed of this welcome dinner for months. For the next week, she and her four girlfriends would cruise the Moselle and Rhine rivers, sailing from Trier, Germany, to Basel, Switzerland. First in line when the doors opened, Adelle headed straight to a table beside the window. The wide floor-to-ceiling windows showcased the red and golden leaves of the trees hugging the shore, their images reflecting in the water.

As the other passengers streamed into the room, Adelle sighed with contentment. The ship would be their home away from home for the next week. Having cruised with this company twice before, she knew they would be treated to delicious meals and interesting ports of call. Best of all, she would be sharing the experience with her girlfriends, like one big happy family. After two busy days in Paris, the five of them had traveled to Trier that day and were now excited to start their river

cruise. Adelle was looking forward to a more leisurely
pace.

"You're in my chair."

A familiar indignant voice jolted Adelle.

Anyone else would have been offended by the
younger woman's tone and hands-on-hips posture.
Instead, Adelle just laughed as she stood up to allow
Barb to get past. During this trip, Adelle was determined
not to worry so much about everything. She would try
harder to understand Barb better and not be so intimidated by her. After all, Barb could be a lot of fun when
she felt like it.

Tilly was right behind Barb. "Adelle, have you
forgotten already?" she asked as she slid past Adelle.
"Barb always sits in the seat facing the entrance." She
sat down beside Barb and winked at Adelle. "Remember, behavior is consistent and therefore predictable."

It still amazed Adelle that Barb and Tilly had
become such good friends. In her seventies, Tilly was
old enough to be Barb's grandmother, great-grand-
mother in fact. But it wasn't just their age that made
them different. Barb lived in the big city; Tilly lived on
a farm. Barb worshipped technology; Tilly resented it.
Barb carried her cellphone at all times; Tilly always
had her craft bag. On their first river cruise, Tilly had
made fidget quilts. On their second trip, she knit
comfort dolls. This time she planned to hand-stitch
small hexagonal pieces to make quilts to go with the
comfort dolls. Barb, on the other hand, spent most of
her time focusing on her phone and her career. And yet,

2

they always seemed to enjoy each other's quiet company.

"Age before beauty, Sis," Debbie sang as she took her customary seat beside Tilly, her older sister.

Tilly smirked. "Beauty was a horse."

Debbie laughed and playfully punched Tilly's shoulder.

Adelle envied the easygoing relationship between the sisters. They made it a practice to travel together regularly, leaving all their everyday responsibilities behind. Adelle desperately wanted to be included in their future trips. She understood what it meant to take off all her other hats - wife, mother, grandmother, and simply enjoy what she wanted to do on her own schedule, with her family of girlfriends. It wasn't that she wanted to get away from her husband, Wes. She loved and appreciated him more each passing year, even though there was one issue that kept her awake some nights.

Not now, Adelle reminded herself. *You promised you wouldn't think about that on this trip.*

Adelle looked around the ship's restaurant for the last woman in their group. "Has anyone seen Teresa?" she asked.

"She's visiting with passengers in the lounge," Debbie said. "As usual."

Tilly rolled her eyes. "Hello, Pot. Look who's calling the kettle black."

Adelle laughed. Tilly was right. Debbie was as outgoing as Teresa. Perhaps more. Debbie loved to be in

3

the spotlight. Tonight, she was dressed in a bright pink peasant blouse, matching pink and green flouncy skirt, and green strappy sandals. Her multi-colored bracelets tinkled as she talked with her hands. She was a living wind chime.

How does Debbie match her lipstick to each outfit? Adelle wondered. *Each and every time?*

"Here comes Teresa now," Barb said.

As Teresa sat down, Adelle noticed her group's reflection in the ship's window. Teresa's auburn hair fell stylishly to her shoulders, while Barb's blonde hair was pulled back in a ponytail. Tilly's short white hair contrasted with her sister's thick wavy blonde curls. Finally, Adelle saw her own reflection. Short gray hair, glasses, and a wide smile. She was in her happy place, traveling with her girlfriends again.

Teresa tapped her wine glass lightly with her fork.

"Do you want us to kiss?" Tilly asked, smirking.

"Pardon?" Teresa asked.

"At the wedding dinners back home, when the guests want the bride and groom to kiss, someone will tap their water glass," Tilly replied. "Then everyone gets in on the action until the deed is done."

Teresa laughed, blew Tilly a kiss, and raised her glass. "To 'the girls.' It's great to river cruise with you again."

Everyone looked pleased as they toasted their success in solving the mystery on their previous trip, except Barb, who was frowning, studying her menu.

"Barb, you should try the regional menu for a

change," Adelle suggested. The *vol-au-vent de champignons* looked delicious. She loved cream. And mushrooms. And pastry. Especially pastry. "Trust me. You'll like it."

A corner of Barb's mouth turned up. "Trust you?"

Tilly snorted. "As in 'trust me, I'll give you a wake-up call'?"

Everyone burst out laughing. 'Trust me' had become a standing joke. Adelle was relieved that everyone had a sense of humor. It wasn't her fault that she forgot to set her alarm that morning. Okay, maybe it *was* her fault. Details weren't her strength. Fortunately, Barb had set her own cellphone alarm. When no one showed up at breakfast, she had roused everyone in time to gulp down breakfast before scrambling to catch the motorcoach from Paris to Trier.

"That's okay," Debbie said. "You're forgiven." She raised her glass. "To Adelle, the best tour host ever!"

That really got the girls laughing, including Adelle. They all knew that Adelle was their tour host in title only. The river cruise company took care of everything. All Adelle had to do was relax and enjoy the trip.

As her friends studied their menus, Adelle felt grateful for the circumstances that had brought them together. After retirement, she was bored. Then fate intervened. Her travel agent friend asked her to fill in as a last-minute tour host, accompanying sisters and two solo women who had booked a river cruise from Budapest to Amsterdam. Thankfully, Adelle had said yes. After bonding while solving the disappearance of diamonds onboard the first cruise, the five women had eagerly booked a second trip together, from Lyon to Avignon. Unfortunately, Teresa had missed that cruise, but now the five women were reunited for another trip.

Peeking over the top of her menu, Adelle noticed that Barb was still slumped in her chair, scowling at her cellphone. She looked miserable. Now that she thought of it, Adelle realized that she had not seen Barb smile once since they had all met in Paris two days ago. There was the odd smirk, but that was it. Adelle began to worry. Barb hadn't answered either of Adelle's chatty emails leading up to their cruise. Had she inadvertently offended Barb? Was that why Barb had spent all of her time with Teresa and Tilly in Paris and none with her?

Don't be so sensitive, she chided herself. *She's the same aloof woman she has always been.*

Adelle decided to loosen Barb up a bit. Thinking for a moment, she came up with a topic sure to coax a smile from their young friend. She would ask Barb about her career. That always made her happy. "Barb, you haven't told us how things are going at work."

Barb looked up and glared at Adelle.

Uh-oh...

Adelle tried not to wince when Teresa kicked her under the table. She made a mental note to question Teresa about Barb later.

"Has everyone heard about the nightly trivia contest?" Teresa asked.

Debbie clapped her hands. "Tilly and I love trivia contests!"

6

"Especially when we win," Tilly said.

As the sisters shared stories of previous victories, Adelle had an idea. Maybe pitching in to win the trivia contests was something she could do to earn her way on to future trips with the girls. All she had to do was pay more attention to the daily excursions. *No problem,* thought Adelle. *You've got this.*

Adelle turned her attention to the desserts listed at the bottom of her menu. Should she order the butterscotch tart? Or the regional specialty, *Moelleux au Chocolat*? She didn't know what *moelleux* meant, but anything with chocolate must be good!

———

It was a beautiful sunny morning as they began their walking tour of Trier. Their ship docked near the town center, and Adelle enjoyed their stroll past charming cafes along the Moselle River.

"It's so peaceful here," said Teresa walking beside Adelle. "And quiet, relative to Paris."

Adelle agreed. She had enjoyed their two days in Paris, but they were so busy sightseeing that she felt she hadn't had enough one-on-one time with her friends. Adelle finally had the opportunity to chat with Teresa. It was time to reconnect. And find out what was up with Barb.

"I'm so happy you could join us this time," Adelle said. "We missed you on our last trip."

"It seems like ages since we traveled together," Teresa said.

Teresa filled Adelle in on the business she was running with her son. "I think he was happy to get rid of me," Teresa said. She chuckled. "He practically pushed me out the car door at the airport. He knows how much I enjoy cruising with all of you."

Adelle remembered saying goodbye to Wes at the airport. After months of working in his home office, he was eager to get to the farm to help his friend with the harvest. He hadn't pushed her out of his truck, but he hadn't lingered either. Adelle hoped he would reconsider her wishes.

Enough, Adelle. Pay attention to the guide.

Their local tour guide told them that Trier was the oldest town in Germany, dating back to 15 BC. As they came up to the High Cathedral of Saint Peter, known as the Trier Cathedral, Teresa stopped abruptly.

"Incredible," Teresa said as she studied the cathedral in awe.

Adelle had forgotten how passionate Teresa was about European architecture. When the guide mentioned that the cathedral was listed as a UNESCO World Heritage Site, Teresa beamed. She had a bucket list to visit as many listed sites as possible.

In Paris, Teresa had crossed another site off her list. She had taken Tilly and Barb on an excursion to the Palace of Versailles. Listening to the three of them talking about the palace tour afterward, Adelle felt she had gone with them even though she and Debbie had gone shopping instead. Teresa described all the reasons the palace had been listed as a World Heritage Site, primarily for its seventeenth-century architecture and art. The palace had been built by King Louis XIV, who had lived in the Louvre in the center of Paris. Feeling hemmed in by the surrounding buildings, he wanted something bigger and more impressive, so he decided to renovate the family's hunting lodge in Versailles.

Although it reminded Adelle of her renovation woes with Wes, the story fascinated her. The lodge's expansion was a considerable undertaking as the area was surrounded by swamps that had to be drained. The marshy fields were transformed into gardens enhanced by fountains boasting sophisticated water effects. King Louis wanted hundreds of fountains, so artificial ponds were created, aqueducts were built, and nearby waters were redirected to the palace. But it was still not enough. The fountains were activated and deactivated whenever the King promenaded in the gardens to keep up the illusion that everything was working fine. More water was needed, so new techniques and hydraulics were invented to pump water from the Seine River. Since the King's main goal was to impress, no expense was too much.

The Palace's *Galerie des Glaces*, the Hall of Mirrors, had been Tilly's favorite tour highlight. She had teased Debbie that the 357 mirrors had been installed just for her. "Too bad you went shopping with Adelle instead," she had said. Adelle silently agreed. She had reluctantly said yes when Debbie joked that a "good tour host" would go with her to the shops along the Champs-Elysees instead of the Palace of Versailles. Adelle had taken one for the team and spent the afternoon with Debbie. She got to experience shopping twice – first when Debbie dragged her from shop to shop, and then again when she shared every Parisienne fashion trend at the dinner table that night.

Enough moaning about shopping, Adelle. Let it go.

Teresa was fascinated by the architectural details of the Trier Cathedral, while Adelle focused on its history.

The cathedral was commissioned by the first Christian Emperor, Constantine the Great, in 326 AD to celebrate the twentieth year of his reign. To mark the occasion, he also began the construction of St. Peter's Basilica in Rome. The Trier Cathedral was destroyed when the Franks invaded the Western Roman Empire in the fifth century. It was rebuilt and mostly destroyed again by the Vikings in the ninth century. In 1035, the surviving remnant of Constantine's church was enlarged in the Romanesque style.

Teresa pointed out every detail of the Gothic and Baroque touches added later.

Adelle was relieved when Barb and the sisters joined them. It was time for another topic. She asked the girls if they thought Reims would be mentioned in the trivia contest.

"Did everyone see the smiling sculpture on the Cathedral of Notre-Dame?" Teresa asked, referring to the cathedral they had toured in Reims on their way to Trier.

"Yes," Debbie replied. "It reminded me of you, Adelle."

"Little Miss Pollyanna," Adelle overheard Barb mutter to Tilly.

Pollyanna? Adelle bristled. *What an insult!*

Fortunately, Wes came to mind before Adelle said something she would later regret. "Insult?" he would ask, laughing at her. "Lighten up, pumpkin."

Okay. Maybe she was overreacting. Adelle took a deep breath and reminded herself that she wanted to get along better with Barb. "I didn't notice that particular sculpture," she replied.

"That's not a surprise," Debbie said, giggling. "There were hundreds of statues."

"Over two thousand three hundred statues," Tilly said.

Adelle sighed. Ever since Teresa had mentioned the nightly trivia games in the lounge, Tilly had become even more attentive to every detail. Every single detail. *It must be exhausting!*

"I took a picture of the angel," Debbie said, passing her phone to Adelle. The angel looked so sweet and cheery. Adelle could almost see a twinkle in her eyes.

"The Reims cathedral is the only Gothic cathedral to display angel statues with open wings," Teresa said. "The smiling angel sculpture is especially unique because stone statues of the period normally didn't have facial expressions."

"Like the stone faces on most big-city folk these days," Tilly said.

Debbie chuckled. "Hello, Pot. Have you ever looked in the mirror before your first coffee of the day?"

"*Touché*," Tilly replied.

Teresa told them that the smiling angel was believed to give hope, belief, and the power of recovery.

Not a bad legacy, thought Adelle. *For a medieval Pollyanna.*

Teresa stopped mid-step as they approached a large, ancient Roman structure. Adelle almost walked into her. Again.

"This is the famous Porta Nigra, which is Latin for 'black gate,'" their guide said. "It was built using grey sandstone around 170 AD. A chemical reaction caused the sandstone to darken, thus its name."

Adelle stood back and admired the dark twin gateways with the high arches. They were protected from above by two levels of defense galleries and two circular towers on either side; one three stories high and the other four stories in height.

"You are looking at the best-preserved Roman city gate north of the Alps," the guide said proudly. "It was built using approximately seventy-two hundred blocks of stone, some weighing as much as six metric tons."

The group followed the guide through one of the enormous rounded arches as he continued the tour.

"Trier was established as a Roman colony in the first century AD. In the second century, it was a great trading center. By the third century, it had become known as the second Rome. This is the only Roman gate that remains in Trier. The other three were gradually pillaged for their stone and iron."

"There are modern-day pillagers back home," Tilly said, scowling as they explored the site. "We have an old abandoned barn on our farm. Last summer, we caught a fellow trespassing. He had a crowbar with him and was determined to pry away weathered boards for a feature wall in his new house."

"Without asking?" Adelle asked. She couldn't believe anyone would be so brazen.

"Yes," Tilly replied. "He had quite the nerve. When we said he couldn't trespass and take barn wood from our property without permission, he offered to pay us." Tilly crossed her arms. "He didn't understand. Even though the barn is no longer in use, it's still part of our family history. We sent him away empty-handed."

Tilly ranted about all the heritage buildings that had been torn down "in the name of progress."

"Take our grain elevators, for example," she said. "Every small town used to have at least one elevator. They had character. Now they've been torn down and replaced by ugly cement towers." Tilly grimaced. "Young people these days have no sense of history and tradition."

Debbie patted her sister's arm. "Not everything can remain the same, Sis. That old barn is a fire hazard. You can't even store anything in it anymore. At least you could get some money from salvaging and selling the old wood."

"Life isn't always about money," Tilly said before stomping away.

Debbie turned to Adelle. "Sorry about that. Tilly is still struggling with change. Her son has taken over the farm. He's started to modernize the operation to increase profits, and she doesn't like it. Especially since she can't operate any of the new computerized equipment."

Adelle felt sorry for Tilly. She knew what it was like to feel pushed aside by technology. Before she had retired, computer advancements had rapidly transformed the investment industry. She couldn't keep up. Just when she caught on to new systems and software, the technology changed. She was continually learning new tools, which took time away from doing what she loved: meeting with her clients. Tilly's resistance reminded Adelle of something Mark Twain supposedly said, 'I'm all for progress, it's change I don't like.'

Adelle thought about change versus progress as the walking tour continued. She loved variety and anything new. Wes, however, loved stability and tradition. She agreed with the saying that opposites attract, but it didn't mean they were always on the same page. Sometimes there was tension. Adelle and Wes had learned to compromise, but now Adelle felt like she was giving in most of the time. All of their friends were renovating and updating their homes while their own house became more and more dated each year. It had become a contentious issue. Wes had dug in. And Adelle had started to feel resentful.

Enough. Adelle, you're on vacation. Focus on the

guide.

"The Porta Nigra is all that remains of the Roman walls built around Trier during the reign of Marcus Aurelius. He was Emperor between 161 – 180 AD. It was a peaceful time here. This gate gave access to a colonnaded road suggesting that rather than defense, the main purpose of Porta Nigra was to impress visitors."

Adelle was impressed that the gate was still standing almost two thousand years later.

"Marcus Aurelius was known as the last of the Five Good Emperors of Rome. Unfortunately, the end of his reign also marked the end of a period of internal tranquility and good government."

Internal tranquility.

Adelle liked that phrase. She wanted to experience more internal tranquility.

Their guide pointed up to the many openings used for catapults. It may have been a peaceful time, Adelle thought, but the Romans were prepared in case it didn't last.

"After the Roman Empire fell," the guide said, "they used the city gate for a variety of purposes. In the eleventh century, it served for seven years as the humble residence of a hermit monk named Simeon. When he died, the gate was converted into a church, saving it from being destroyed. When Napoleon saw Porta Nigra in 1804, he demanded that the church be dissolved, and the gate be restored to its original ancient Roman design."

Tilly poked Adelle in the ribs. "Even Napoleon had

a sense of tradition," she whispered.

Strolling around the enormous gate, Adelle found herself beside Barb in the small inner courtyard.

"This is where raiders and invaders were trapped and covered in tar," Barb said menacingly.

Was it her imagination, or had Barb emphasized the phrase 'raiders and invaders'? Adelle flinched, recalling Barb's glare when she had asked her about her job at dinner the night before. Perhaps Barb thought Adelle was invading her privacy. Then she remembered the unanswered chatty emails she had sent Barb before the trip. She was sure she had asked her about her career then as well. And then there was the Pollyanna comment. What was that all about?

Adelle couldn't wait to leave the threatening court-yard and corner Teresa. Since she was sharing a cabin with Barb, perhaps she would know why Barb was so ornery.

When the morning walking tour ended, the sisters and Barb returned to the ship. Adelle invited Teresa to stay and have coffee at one of the quaint cafes along the Moselle River. Roman history and Barb's unnerving comment had reminded Adelle of one of the expressions she had learned in school. *Carpe diem*. It was time to seize the day and ask Teresa why she had kicked her under the table the previous night.

As they ordered coffee, Adelle was distracted when

an elderly couple sat down at one of the outdoor tables. The man wore a black fedora with a white band and red feather, pulled down low over his sunglasses. She was shocked when the man pocketed the coins that had obviously been left for a tip. Adelle instinctively felt the money belt tucked inside her slacks. *Better safe than sorry.*

Teresa cleared her throat. "I'm sorry I kicked you last night," Teresa said. "It just wasn't the time or place to talk about what has happened to Barb." Her expression alarmed Adelle.

"Barb is embarrassed. She's lost her job."

Teresa explained that Barb's company had been taken over by a corporate raider who was breaking the company up and selling it off. Barb's special investigation unit had been disbanded.

Barb's menacing comment in the courtyard suddenly made sense. Adelle rankled at the unfairness. Barb had been one hundred percent devoted and loyal to her employer. "She shouldn't be embarrassed; it's not her fault!"

"True," Teresa agreed. "But she's not ready to let anyone know her circumstances yet."

"When did Barb find out?" Adelle asked.

"She just heard about the takeover three days ago. This morning she received official notice."

Adelle felt sorry for Barb. Her career meant everything to her, and she had worked so hard to get her promotions.

"It's going to take a while for Barb to find a similar

position," Teresa said. "Her analytical and technological skills are very specialized."

Adelle agreed. Every time anyone asked Barb what she did for a living, she replied that they wouldn't understand. It had become another standing joke.

"Barb is low on funds," Teresa continued. "I've offered to help her, but she won't let me. You know how proud and independent she is."

That's an understatement, Adelle thought, reflecting on Barb's financial circumstances.

Teresa had wanted to pay Barb for solving the mystery of the missing funds during the last cruise, but Barb had declined. She had insisted that a cash payment would contravene company policy. Adelle had suggested Teresa invite Barb to share a cabin this trip and use frequent flyer points for Barb's flights. All the trip had cost Barb was a little bit of her pride. She relented after Adelle told her that it was important to let people thank her.

"She's low in funds?" Adelle had always coached her clients to have at least six months' emergency funds in reserve. Most people, however, lived from paycheck to paycheck.

Barb wasn't one of them. She had just moved into a new condo, Teresa explained.

"She showed me her budget spreadsheet," Teresa said. "She had it all figured out." Teresa let out a worried sigh. "Now she's worried about bankruptcy."

Bankruptcy? Adelle felt nauseous. "Is there anything I can do?"

Teresa stirred her coffee. "Maybe. I think there is a situation coming up that looks promising."

"A situation?" Adelle asked. Teresa was well connected in the business world. Perhaps her connections could help.

"I can't say anything more at this point," Teresa said. "But we might need your help. I'm waiting for confirmation of a conference call tomorrow morning. Barb and I might have to miss the castle excursion."

Adelle was disappointed. The tour of Reichsburg Castle promised to be very interesting.

"Debbie and Tilly will probably wonder where we are," Teresa said. "Can you cover for us?"

It was a simple request, and yet Adelle felt uneasy. She was thrilled that Teresa trusted her enough to share Barb's circumstances. But leaving the sisters out felt wrong. They were part of the group and deserved to know what was going on.

Adelle cringed as she imagined Tilly demanding to know where Barb and Teresa were. "What should I say?"

"You'll think of something," Teresa said, signaling their waiter. "It's time to get back to the ship."

"Thanks for trusting me," Adelle said, getting up from the table. Now that she understood Barb's career and financial status, she was determined to help. She resolved to do the right thing when the time came. She just hoped she would know what the right thing was.

After lunch, Adelle was grateful for the walking track around the top deck of the ship. She needed time to think. If necessary, how would she explain Teresa and Barb's absence tomorrow morning? Should she be honest with the sisters? Or should she cover for Barb? She also needed time to burn off some calories. If only she could avoid eating so many desserts. When she couldn't decide between the *crème brûlée* or the *profiteroles*, their server had brought her a generous serving of each!

The ship sailed past vineyard after vineyard, village after quaint village, and campground after campground as they cruised down the beautiful Moselle River.

"Isn't the scenery gorgeous?"

Startled, Adelle tripped as she turned toward the woman who had joined her on the track.

"Sorry," the woman said, reaching out to steady her. "I didn't mean to scare you."

Following introductions, the women resumed their walk.

"This ship is like a floating boutique hotel," Jan said. "No suitcases to pack and unpack each day, no meals to plan, exercise in the fresh air, and arriving in a new location every day. Delightful." It was Jan's first river cruise, and she was enjoying it immensely. She and her husband, Sandy, had been pleasantly surprised when Sandy's manager had surprised him with the river cruise as a reward for his dedicated service.

"Sandy started with the company right out of high school." Jan laughed. "I think he was attracted by the company's name. The plumber who started it called it Pipedream Plumbing Supplies."

How appropriate!

Jan explained how Sandy had worked his way up over the past thirty-three years from the warehouse to the office.

"We thought we would be retired before we would be in a position to take a vacation like this," Jan said.

"Sounds like Sandy deserves it," Adelle said. "It's rare to find someone who has stayed with one company for that long."

"He loves his work. And antique cars. He's either at the office or in his garage tinkering with an old car." Jan groaned. "Did you notice all the old cars in Reims?"

Adelle admitted that cars weren't her thing. Wes was always teasing her that the only detail she usually noticed was their color.

"I lost Sandy on our walking tour of Reims. Then I saw a collection of antique cars parked near the town square. Sure enough, there he was."

Jan stopped walking and squinted at her watch. Again.

"Are you concerned about the time?"

Jan laughed. "No, I'm keeping track of my steps. I'm competing with my girlfriend to see who can get the most steps each day." She scanned the upper deck. "I promised Sandy I wouldn't count steps on this trip. It drives him crazy, but what he doesn't know won't hurt him."

Adelle laughed. *True!*

CHAPTER 2
BERNKASTEL

WHERE THERE IS A WILL

The ship arrived in Bernkastel just as the passengers were finishing dinner. Adelle suggested that the five women stroll through the village together. Perhaps it would distract Barb. Now that Adelle knew about her job loss, she couldn't stop worrying about her. Barb's career meant everything to her. She was intelligent, ambitious, and conscientious. *And unemployed. And broke.* Adelle hoped that Teresa's connections would help Barb get a new job.

Adelle jumped to the side to avoid getting smacked when Debbie flung her arms wide, bracelets flashing in the setting sun. "This is one of the prettiest towns I've ever seen," Debbie gushed. Adelle agreed as they walked down a cobblestone street. Soon they found themselves in the historic market square surrounded by dozens of tall narrow houses, their white plaster criss-crossed by brownish-red timber above street-level shops on the main floors. Other hilly cobblestone streets radiated out from the square lined with similar homes.

"These are known as half-timbered houses," Teresa said. "The builders worked directly with logs and trees rather than pre-cut lumber. They used broadaxes and other woodworking tools to square the logs off before they carefully joined the timbers with large wooden pegs."

The houses reminded Adelle of illustrations she had seen in fairy tale books.

"Most of these houses date back to the seventeenth century," Tilly said. "Some are even older."

Adelle grinned. After Barb had taught her how to use the internet, Tilly had started to research each destination in advance. "To better prepare for the trivia contest," she had said in response to Debbie's teasing.

"Look at the narrow base of that house," Debbie said, staring across the street. "I doubt if you could fit a kitchen table on the first floor."

The second story and the tall, sharply-peaked attic were hanging over the first floor on three sides.

Tilly consulted her notepad. "It's called the Pointed House. It was built in 1416 and is one of the oldest structures in Bernkastel."

Of course, Debbie needed to get a picture of the group standing in front of the house. It was a good thing the digital revolution had arrived, Adelle thought. Debbie must have taken hundreds of pictures since their trip began. Adelle smiled to herself when Tilly volunteered to take the photo. Tilly hated getting her own picture taken.

"Miss Architect, do you know why these houses are so narrow?" Tilly asked Teresa as the women lined up in front of the house.

Adelle wondered if Teresa was amused or annoyed by the nickname. Tilly knew that Teresa's son was the architect, not her. There seemed to be some tension brewing between Tilly and Teresa. At dinner, they had debated heatedly about urban renewal. It all started when Tilly brought up an email she had received from her friend who lived in a small town near Tilly's farm. The town administrator had erected a "for sale" sign on a vacant lot on the main street.

"I'm so mad; I'm just fumigating!" Tilly had spluttered, causing Adelle to cough into her napkin.

Teresa had suggested that a developer could build on the lot, providing employment and services for their community. Adelle couldn't understand why Tilly was so against the idea until she remembered their conversation from their previous trip.

"Tilly, didn't you spearhead a small park on that lot?" Adelle had asked.

"Yes," Tilly had replied. "After our river cruise in France, some friends and I turned that run-down lot into a local gathering place." She had passed her phone around their table so that everyone could see the pictures of the small park with the well-kept lawn, benches, shrubs, and flowers.

"Look what we did to the wall of the adjacent building," Tilly had said, sharing another photo.

Adelle admired the colorful mural of the Northern Lights.

"Why would the administration want to sell the lot?" Adelle had asked. "Your park is so appealing."

"Money," Tilly replied, jutting out her chin. "The project didn't cost the town a penny. Our costs were covered by donations, and we have a group of volunteers who take care of the maintenance. My friend said they are selling it to top up the town's financial resources."

"Tell them what you told your friend to do," Debbie had prompted.

"I told her that we can't just stand around and do nothing. If we want something, we have to do something." Tilly's eyes narrowed. "I told her to hide the sign in the bushes until I get back. I'll think of something by then."

Adelle felt sorry for Tilly, but she admired her determination. There must be a way that the park could be saved.

As the women lined up for the picture, instead of answering Tilly's question, Teresa repeated it.

"Why are the houses narrow, Tilly?"

"To avoid taxes," Tilly answered triumphantly. "When these were built, taxes were calculated by width and length. So, creative owners built their properties skyward."

Debbie laughed. "Where there is a will, there is always a way."

Tilly handed Debbie's phone back. "Does anyone see the rat house?"

"Rat house?" Adelle asked, cringing as she scanned the town square.

"Rathaus," Debbie translated, spelling it out after laughing at Tilly's pronunciation. "The German word for town hall."

"Rathaus, rat house," Tilly said, eyes twinkling. "Same thing, only different." She pointed at a four-story building. "There it is. See the coat of arms on the second level? The lower floor has been converted into a restaurant and pub."

"The coral paint color makes it look so cheerful," Debbie said.

Adelle agreed. Paint could do wonders. *Enough, Adelle.*

Most of the shops were closed for the evening, but that didn't stop the girls from admiring the cuckoo clocks and carved toy soldiers in one of the shop windows. Suddenly Adelle realized that she had once again forgotten to set the alarm on her cellphone. They were going to miss the trivia contest.

The sisters were gracious in their disappointment, but still, Adelle felt bad that she had let them down. She resolved to make it up to them by being extra diligent about excursion details for the rest of the trip. *How hard could it be?*

On the walk back to the ship, Teresa pulled Adelle

aside. "I've heard from my contact," Teresa said. "Barb and I have a call tomorrow morning. We won't be at breakfast. We need you to cover for us."

Adelle's stomach clenched as she imagined the awkward conversation with Tilly and Debbie. She dreaded the moment.

Reaching the ship, Adelle was still agonizing about what she would say at breakfast when she looked up to see Jan waving from the ship's railing. Seeing her new friend gave her an idea.

"Enjoy your bike excursion tomorrow morning," Adelle told Teresa and Barb as the women were saying goodnight.

Barb looked up at Adelle and winced. *She's probably remembering how stiff and sore she was after cycling on their first trip.*

"What bike excursion?" Debbie asked.

Adelle struggled to look relaxed. "Teresa reminded me that she and Barb are going on the optional bike excursion tomorrow morning. We'll see them again at lunch."

Adelle walked to her cabin, pleased with her inspired idea. What the sisters didn't know wouldn't hurt them.

CHAPTER 3
COCHEM
MISSION ACCOMPLISHED

Adelle looked down from the gate of the Reichsburg Castle perched on the steep hill overlooking the Moselle River and the medieval town of Cochem below.

"Cochem is the most picturesque town I have ever seen," Debbie gushed as she took photos with her phone.

"You said that about Bernkastel," Tilly said, winking at Adelle.

"I know," Debbie admitted, swiveling to get a panoramic shot. "This cruise just keeps getting better."

Adelle couldn't agree more. She was enjoying everything about their trip. She met interesting passengers, savored each meal, got lots of fresh air and exercise, and slept like a baby.

"We should have brought our binoculars," Tilly said, eyeing the river valley below. "Maybe we could have spotted Teresa and Barb on their bikes."

Just like the river mist that morning, Adelle's good

mood evaporated. For a moment, she considered telling the sisters the truth. Why had she made up the bike excursion story? It wasn't like her to outright lie. Honesty was important to her. She needed to remember to think things through before she blurted out the first idea that came into her head. *Now what?* Maybe telling them the truth now would make the situation better, but what if it made the situation worse? What if Barb's call didn't result in anything? Then Adelle would have admitted lying for nothing. She took a deep breath and tried to relax.

"Why don't I take a picture of the two of you standing beside the castle gate?" Adelle offered, changing the topic.

"That would be great," Debbie said, handing Adelle her cellphone. "Sis, smile for a change, and don't forget to pinch the back of my neck."

Adelle laughed. The sisters were full of tricks. They had taught Adelle how to eliminate 'turkey neck' by standing side-by-side and pulling the skin taut on the back of each other's neck. It worked every time.

The guide signaled that it was time to start their tour.

The Reichsburg Castle was originally built in the eleventh century and was used mainly as a defense structure. Adelle imagined the bedlam as forty thousand knights congregated in the same area at the same time.

"In 1294," the guide continued, "the reigning king had pawned the castle and surrounding area to pay for his coronation as German emperor. When neither he nor his successor could redeem the pledge, the archbishops of Trier took over the castle. In the fourteenth century, the archbishop connected the castle to Cochem for protection within its massive walls. Below the castle, a chain was installed to form a removable toll barrier across the Moselle River."

"Another money grab," Tilly hissed.

"In 1689, King Louis XIV, known as the Sun King, ordered his troops to set the castle on fire and blow it up. His troops almost completely destroyed the town of Cochem as well. The castle remained in ruins until 1868. At that time, it was trendy for the nobility and the wealthy to refurbish castle ruins as family summer residences. The castle was purchased by a businessman from Berlin, Louis Ravené, who started to rebuild the castle in the architectural style of the day, neo-gothic."

'Neo-gothic' reminded Adelle of Teresa. *Too bad she had missed the morning tour*, Adelle thought. She hoped Barb's call was successful.

"Since 1978, the castle has been owned by the town of Cochem," the guide said. "Follow me."

The various rooms of the castle were well preserved with Renaissance and Baroque furniture that had been carefully collected by the Ravené family. Wes would have loved all the wood, thought Adelle. Wood-paneled walls, solid wood furniture, high inlaid-wood ceilings, ornate wood carvings, carved wooden archways, and railings. Their own house was full of oak. Oak kitchen cabinets, oak furniture, oak baseboards, and antique oak frames displaying photos of Wes's adored great-grandfather and other pioneers of his generation. Oak was so out of date now, Adelle thought. She wanted to upgrade their home by painting over their oak kitchen cabinets, but Wes was adamant that they stay the same. Adelle bristled. *It may be his castle, but it's my home, too.*

"What are you frowning about?" Debbie asked.

Adelle hadn't realized that she was frowning. She mentally parked her marital disagreement. "Look at her," she said, pointing at a Renaissance painting of a plump reclining nude woman. "Why couldn't we have been born when full figures were the trend?"

Many more double portions of dessert, and you'll hope that trend comes back, Adelle.

Continuing their tour through the castle, their guide motioned the group to be quiet as they walked past a roped-off area. Adelle was surprised to see a small chapel with a wedding in progress. She hoped the bride knew how to stand her ground.

For goodness' sake! Let it go, Adelle!

The sun shone brightly as the tour group followed their guide from the castle down to the bustling streets of Cochem. Strolling along, he pointed out the Moselle slate tiles on the tall, gabled, half-timbered houses.

"The slate soils on the steep slopes above Cochem are also well suited for vineyards," the guide said. Tilly took notes as the guide told them that the vineyard owners grew mostly Riesling grapes, a white variety that made up about 60% of the Moselle region. The long exposure to sunshine was beneficial for the Riesling grapes since they ripened late in the season, producing fruity wines with layers of flavor.

Adelle waved to a bride and groom seated in the back of a red convertible driving down the main street. She recognized them as the couple she had seen at the castle.

Uh-oh…

Was that Teresa and Barb further down the street? She needed to quickly distract the sisters. "Debbie, Tilly, look at all the Riesling wine in this shop," she said, pointing at the shop window beside them. "Let's pop in and buy some local wine for happy hour on the deck this afternoon."

Adelle was relieved when they came back out of the shop. *Mission accomplished.* Teresa and Barb were nowhere to be seen.

"How was your bike ride this morning?" Tilly asked as Adelle and the sisters joined Teresa and Barb for lunch in the ship's restaurant.

Barb smirked at Adelle but said nothing.

Adelle looked at Teresa, silently pleading with her to say something. *Anything.*

"It was a beautiful morning for a bike ride," Teresa said.

"It was also a great day for our tour, too," said

Adelle. "Debbie, you should show Teresa and Barb your pictures of our excursion."

"Who is this dapper gentleman in the last picture? Teresa said, pointing to Debbie's phone screen.

"His name is Andreas," Debbie replied. "At the end of our morning walking tour, our guide took us to a local winery."

"Andreas owns the winery," Tilly chimed in. "We got to taste three different family products. The first was a Riesling prosecco, then a 'classic Riesling,' followed by a liqueur with a long German name that I can't begin to pronounce."

"Andreas said the name roughly translates to red little peach liqueur," said Debbie.

"He told us that the sweet liqueur is made from tiny red 'vineyard peaches,'" Tilly added. "The ancient Romans introduced peaches to the Cochem area, and they have grown alongside the grapevines ever since."

Debbie shared one of the amusing local legends that Andreas had told them.

"Long ago, a mob threatened Cochem. They found the gates locked, so they camped out in the meadow and prepared to attack the town the next day. One of the town councilors ordered everyone to roll empty wine barrels up to the gateway and pile them high. When the mob prepared to storm the town the next morning, the citizens pushed over the pyramid, and the barrels tumbled down the hill straight into the ranks of the attackers."

Barb snorted. "A real mob wouldn't be deterred by a few empty wine barrels."

"She's not done yet," Tilly said.

"What happened next?" Teresa asked.

"They withdrew their attack," Debbie replied. She chuckled. "They decided that a town with that many empty wine barrels wouldn't have enough full barrels worth looting."

"Good point," Barb conceded.

"The story gave me an idea," Adelle said. "Tilly, maybe your friend can somehow find out whenever prospective buyers are in town to look at your lot. Before they arrive, your friend could throw empty bottles around the park, dissuading them from buying it."

Everyone laughed at Adelle's idea, and that was okay. She had often told them that she wasn't attached to her ideas. Some were good, some were iffy, and some were downright terrible. They all knew she would soon come up with another one anyway.

Back to the drawing board, Adelle.

"Teresa, I thought I saw you and Barb in the town square after our castle tour," Debbie said, scanning her menu. "Before I could wave you over, Adelle distracted us."

Uh-oh...

"We bought some wine for happy hour," Adelle said. "A local Riesling," she added, hoping to sidetrack the sisters again.

"Sounds inviting," Teresa replied. She put her menu

down and grinned at Debbie. "We were done in time to walk around Cochem. There were some lovely shops."

Debbie took the bait.

Teresa is so smooth, Adelle thought as the conversation turned to shopping. Everything she said was the truth.

Adelle surveyed her menu. As much as she would love red bell pepper soup for a first course, she wanted to save room for the chocolate chip sundae. Or the *Parisienne flan*. Or maybe a little of each. Skimming through the main course options, she imagined what Wes would be eating. Likely sandwiches in the field as they harvested the wheat. Definitely not *pappardelle al ragu* or parmesan-crusted veal scaloppini. She tried not to drool.

"Speaking of shopping," Debbie said, "why don't we all spend tomorrow morning in Koblenz together? I've heard the shops there are *magnifique!*" Her bracelets jingled as she kissed her fingers and flung them outward.

Adelle's mouth went dry. Anything but more shopping. She didn't shop at home, and she sure didn't come all the way to Europe to walk aimlessly from store to store.

"Thanks, but I've already agreed to go on the morning excursion with Jan and Sandy," she blurted, reaching for her water glass.

"Is Jan the woman you met on the walking track?" Tilly asked.

Tilly doesn't miss a thing, Adelle reflected later, as

she rushed off after lunch to invite Jan and Sandy to join her on the Koblenz morning excursion.

"Sorry I made other plans for tomorrow morning in Koblenz," Adelle said as she joined Debbie on the ship's deck to enjoy the afternoon scenic sail along the Moselle. She was worried the girls were mad at her for declining the invitation to shop with them.

"That's okay," Debbie replied. "Your new friends are lucky to have an experienced tour host join them."

Adelle felt herself blush. "Thank you," she stammered.

"I wanted to thank *you* for the idea you gave me on our last trip," Debbie said. As they sat down in lounge chairs facing the shoreline, Debbie updated Adelle on her business. Since adding the French bistro-themed café to her women's clothing consignment store, her revenues had more than doubled.

"We've become *the* neighborhood meeting place," Debbie said, eyes shining. "The place to meet old friends and to make new friends."

Like our river cruises, Adelle thought.

"It's been really busy." Debbie laughed. "Thanks to your ideas from our last river cruise, I needed this vacation to recharge!"

"There you are, Sis," Tilly said, arriving with Teresa. "It's time for French lessons in the lounge."

"To improve our brains," Debbie said, winking at

Adelle. "Good thing the lessons include sampling the local wines."

"Which is also good for our brains," Tilly said, locking arms with her sister as they left. "A bean toe."

"A bean toe?" Teresa asked Adelle as she watched them leave. "Did someone stub their toe?"

Adelle laughed. "I think she meant '*a bientôt.*' 'See you later.'"

Teresa chuckled as she settled down in Debbie's vacated lounge chair.

"How did your conference call go this morning?" Adelle burst out as soon as the sisters were out of sight.

"It went very well."

"Who were you speaking with?" Adelle finally asked.

"A businessman I met at a conference six weeks ago," Teresa replied. "During one of our breaks, he overheard me talking about how Barb had done some investigating for me. Last week, he called me to arrange an introduction. This morning, we had an exploratory meeting by video conference call. He explained what the problem was, and Barb explained how she might be able to help him."

Adelle waited to see if Teresa would volunteer any more information. After several excruciating moments, she couldn't help herself. "Did she get the case?"

"Affirmative," Teresa said, mimicking Barb.

With a little more prompting, Teresa shared a little more information. "He wants her to investigate some improprieties in his department."

"While we're on our cruise?" Adelle asked.

"Based on what he told her, Barb said she could examine their accounts remotely. She thinks it will only take a couple of days at the most."

"But why can't she wait until she gets back home?"

"He agreed to auto-deposit Barb's fee as soon as she emailed her findings. She needs to complete the investigation as soon as possible so that she can pay her mortgage payment on time."

Adelle was relieved that Barb had been retained and would be paid immediately. Soon they could all relax and enjoy the rest of their trip together. She visualized their itinerary: Koblenz tomorrow, Mainz the next day. By Speyer, they should be one big happy family again.

"Can we tell Debbie and Tilly what is going on?" Adelle asked hopefully. She felt guilty for misleading them. It wasn't like her to lie. Honesty had been the foundation of her success as a retirement planner. Her clients trusted her. She didn't want to lose the sisters' trust.

"Not yet," Teresa replied. "Barb's client stressed the importance of confidentiality. He was adamant that no one else knows about her investigation." She frowned. "I've probably said too much already."

"Don't worry," Adelle said. "You can trust me. I promise not to say anything."

Just two more days. How hard could it be?

CHAPTER 4
KOBLENZ

COUNTING CHICKENS BEFORE THEY
HATCH

"We changed rivers during the night," Debbie said, standing beside Adelle at the ship's railing. The Moselle merged with the Rhine in Koblenz. Now they were enjoying a morning sail through the Rhine Gorge. Although they had sailed this gorge before, on their river cruise from Budapest to Amsterdam, Adelle was grateful for the opportunity to do it again. It was so beautiful, and there was so much history to absorb. Teresa had reminded them that the upper Middle Rhine valley was added to the UNESCO list of World Heritage Sites in 2002. Adelle loved the castles, picturesque towns, and vineyards, and she was fascinated by the legends shared by their program director.

This time, Adelle had intended to sit at the bow of the ship, but someone had saved the prime spot hours ago. From time to time, Adelle checked to see who it was.

"Have you met that couple?" she asked Debbie

when a man and woman moved the sweaters and sat down.

"Only once," replied Debbie. "She seems to go out of her way to be miserable. Most of the other passengers have learned to avoid them. Tilly and I call them Mr. and Mrs. Grumpy. She complains about *everything*. It's like she is walking around, waiting to be offended."

What could they possibly complain about, Adelle wondered. Even the weather was cooperating. Back home, Wes wasn't so fortunate. He had texted that rain had delayed the harvest for a few days. He was back in the city, catching up on some of his office work. For a brief moment, Adelle was hopeful. Maybe he would have time to reconsider the first item on her wish list – painting over the oak kitchen cupboards.

"Are you sure you don't want to come shopping with us when we get to Koblenz?" Debbie asked, interrupting her daydream. "It's your last chance."

Last chance to be honest, Adelle.

"Thanks, but I have to pass," Adelle said. "I promised to go with Jan and Sandy."

———

Adelle met Jan and Sandy at the end of the ramp. She looked forward to getting to know them better on the walking tour of Koblenz.

The ship was docked near the Deutsches Eck, the famous German corner where the Moselle and Rhine rivers merged. Adelle looked up at the huge equestrian statue of William I, the first German Emperor. The monument had been erected in appreciation of his role in the unification of Germany.

"Our group was here on our first river cruise, from Budapest to Amsterdam," Adelle told Sandy and Jan. "You're going to love Koblenz."

"Where is the rest of your group?" Jan said, looking around.

"They've done this tour before. Believe it or not, the girls, as I like to call them, went shopping."

Adelle stopped herself from thanking Jan for rescuing her from being dragged along from store to store. As Tilly liked to say, she didn't want Jan and Sandy to feel like they were playing second fiddle.

"We have a different local guide this time." Adelle loved how each guide brought their own personal perspective to each excursion. She looked forward to hearing what their guide, Klaus, would say about Koblenz.

Klaus pointed out the Ehrenbreitstein Fortress at the top of the steep hill across the river. Because the Moselle and Rhine rivers joined together at this location, Koblenz had long been a desirable place to live. The prime site also meant that Koblenz had endured many invaders, including the Romans, the Vikings, the Prussians, and the French. Out of necessity, Koblenz was surrounded by four fortresses, including the Ehrenbreitstein Fortress.

"Two of the girls took the cable car to the fortress the first time we were here," Adelle said. "The rest of our group was touring another fortress, Marksburg Castle."

As they followed Klaus, Adelle remembered how Tilly had scolded Barb for twisting her ankle coming back from Ehrenbreitstein. She had tripped when she was looking at her cellphone instead of where she was going. Thinking of Barb, Adelle's thoughts drifted to an awkward moment earlier that morning.

"Is Barb working on a case?" Debbie had asked Adelle when they had arrived for breakfast before the others. "We really missed her at the lounge last night."

The sisters had been looking forward to teaming up with Barb to win the nightly trivia contest. They were sure that Barb would know the answers to any questions they couldn't answer themselves. They were dismayed when Mr. and Mrs. Grumpy won the competition.

"Teresa told us Barb wouldn't be at breakfast today," Debbie had added.

"Did you ask Teresa why?" Adelle had crossed her fingers under the table.

"No, I assumed you would know." Debbie had grinned. "After all, you're our tour host."

"I don't know what she's working on," Adelle had replied. *That was sort of true.*

Walking with Jan and Sandy, Adelle was relieved to spend the morning with her new friends instead of avoiding more lies with her old friends. It was an easy fifteen-minute stroll along the waterfront to the town center of Koblenz. They arrived at a fountain near the site of the first Roman fortification. The fountain was built in 1992 to commemorate Koblenz's two-thou-sandth anniversary.

"And I thought twenty-nine years was long," Sandy said, teasing Jan about their upcoming wedding anniversary.

As the tour group continued down a romantic street between two churches, stopping at the Basilica of St. Castor, the oldest church in Koblenz, Adelle paid attention. Any information might be important. She hadn't contributed anything to the trivia contest the night before, and she was deter-mined to do better that night. The church was constructed by the Archbishop of Trier between 817 and 836, with the support of Emperor Louis the Pious. Adelle was impressed by the size of the large structure.

"The present-day building dates mainly from the twelfth century," Klaus said. He pointed out an older fountain in the square in front of the basilica. "In 1812, the French prefect, Jules Doazan, had it engraved. He obviously assumed that Napoleon would be victorious in his Russian campaign." Klaus translated the French inscription on the fountain's plaque: 'In 1812/Memorial to the campaign against the Russians/under the prefec-ture of Jules Doazan.'"

Klaus grinned mischievously. "Doazan was wrong. Napoleon's campaign in Russia ended in a devastating defeat. Within two years, the French abandoned Koblenz, leaving without a fight."

Adelle grinned as she imagined what Tilly would

say: "Doazan shouldn't have counted his chickens before they hatched."

"The new city commander could have demolished the fountain," Klaus continued. "Instead, he showed a sense of humor by adding another engraving below the first one."

Klaus translated the second French inscription:

"'Seen and approved by us, the Russian commander of the city of Koblenz, on 1 January 1814.'"

Jan chuckled. "Thus, immortalizing the memory of Napoleon's defeat and the end of French rule in Koblenz. Brilliant."

Continuing their tour, Adelle was glad Klaus was leading their group and not her. She had lost all sense of direction as they followed him through the narrow streets to Jesuit Square, named after the religious order that operated in the area from 1580 to 1773. Klaus pointed out the beautiful old school on the eastern side of the square. Since 1895, it has been used as the Koblenz Town Hall.

"What are you chuckling about now?" Jan asked Adelle.

Adelle told them about Tilly's mispronunciation of Rathaus, the German name for a town hall. "You'll love getting to know her. She is passionate about positive aging."

Adelle shared Tilly's interest in learning other languages in order to keep her mind active. Adelle had bumped into her at the ship's coffee station just that morning. Tilly was irritated at Debbie for waking her up when she returned late from socializing the previous evening. Tilly had grumbled something in French. Adelle had thought she said that Debbie was in court with a hairy coat. Exasperated, Tilly had shown Adelle the phrase she had copied down from their French lesson: "*Elle me court sur le haricot.*"

"She is annoying me," Tilly had translated.

Adelle had struggled not to grin.

"The fool should know better than to gallivant in the lounge all night," Tilly had muttered before she left with her first morning coffee in hand.

Adelle was still laughing to herself.

After a pleasant stroll through more interesting neighborhoods, Klaus stopped in front of a row of cafes and brewhouses. "Time for a break," he said. "We'll regroup at this spot in an hour, and then I will lead you back to your ship."

Sandy suggested sampling a local beer at the charming brewhouse directly across the street. Jan volunteered to watch their time. "6000 steps already," she whispered to Adelle after checking her watch.

Over beer and pretzels, Adelle led the conversation to her favorite topic. She loved to hear about other people's paths in life. Jan had told her a little about Sandy, but Adelle didn't know much about Jan. She found out that Jan volunteered at her local school library. She loved to read, and she loved introducing students to good books.

Adelle thought back to her own childhood. As soon as she had learned how to read, her world had opened up. When her parents started to bring home Little Golden Books with their groceries, Adelle had devoured stories about kittens, puppies, farm animals, and fairy tales. At school, she had discovered libraries. She was still an avid reader.

"Our high school was new with a well-stocked library," Adelle said. "I used to pick a topic and read every book on the shelf about it. Then I would pick another topic and do it again." She had become a life-long learner, always interested in learning new things. Especially where people were involved.

"What was your favorite fiction book as a young child?" Jan asked.

Adelle loved Nancy Drew, the Hardy Boys, Huckleberry Finn, Tom Sawyer… She found it impossible to narrow down the list.

Hearing Sandy yawn, Adelle realized that they had excluded him from the conversation.

"How did you meet each other?" Adelle asked Sandy, changing the topic.

"We were high school sweethearts," Sandy replied. He toasted Jan with his beer stein. "I married the smartest girl in my class."

Jan beamed as she returned the toast. "Smart enough to recognize that Sandy was 'the one' for me."

As they sampled a large pretzel, Adelle asked how they were enjoying their trip.

"Sandy was skeptical about river cruising," Jan began.

"True," Sandy admitted. "I was worried that we

wouldn't know anyone. I thought we would be bored." He laughed. "I was wrong. It's so easy to meet people, and we are certainly not bored!"

"What have you liked the most so far?" Adelle asked, taking another piece of the soft pretzel.

Sandy lit up as he talked about the classic antique cars he had seen in Reims.

"The car owners were on an organized Reims Champagne tour. They stayed in Reims for three nights and visited nearby champagne houses and vineyards during the day."

"What about drinking and driving?" Adelle asked. The beauty of river cruising was the ability to enjoy happy hours, wine-pairing at dinner, and relaxing with a favorite beverage in the lounge in the evenings. Not overdoing it, of course. As Tilly liked to say, everything in moderation, including moderation.

"Their cars mean too much to them to drink and drive," Sandy replied, signaling their waiter for another pretzel.

"I recognized another passenger admiring the cars. He told me about the optional excursion from Mainz tomorrow. It's a tour of the nearby Opel factory."

Sandy was shocked that Adelle had never heard of Opel, one of the world's leading car manufacturers specializing in passenger cars, mini-buses, and light vans. The original company had been founded by Adam Opel as a sewing machine factory. It became Germany's largest car manufacturer in 1928. Sandy was excited about the onsite vintage car collection.

"Are you going on the tour?" Adelle asked, noticing how animated Sandy was.

Jan groaned. Sandy looked crestfallen.

Uh-oh...

"Mainz is also the home of the printing press and the Gutenburg Museum," Jan said, sounding frustrated. "The excursions are at the same time."

Visiting the birthplace of the printing press must be the top item on a booklover's bucket list, Adelle thought. Poor Jan. Sandy was looking off into the distance. Poor Sandy. If only the excursions were at different times.

Suddenly, Adelle had an idea. "Jan, why don't you join the girls and me on the Mainz excursion?"

Sandy sat up and grinned. "That would be awesome! I can go to the Opel factory and relax, knowing that Jan will be in good company."

Jan placed her palm over her heart. "Thanks, Adelle. That would be a dream come true."

After toasting the new plan, the conversation turned to 'the girls.'

"If you are interested in architecture, Teresa is an expert," Adelle said. *Except you might learn more than you bargained for*, she thought. "Tilly and Debbie are sisters. Tilly still lives on a farm in the middle of the prairies. Debbie is twelve years younger, lives on the west coast, and owns a women's clothing consignment store and cafe."

"You mentioned four girlfriends," Jan said. "Who is the other one?"

What should she say about Barb? Adelle wondered. *Keep it simple, Adelle.*

"The youngest woman in our group is in her early thirties. Her name is Barb."

"What does Barb do for a living?" Jan asked.

Adelle blurted the first thing that came to mind. "She's a consultant."

Sandy laughed. "My boss detests consultants. He says all they do is borrow your watch, tell you what time it is, give your watch back to you, and charge you for their time."

"Speaking of time," Jan said, glancing at her watch, "we better drink up and rejoin Klaus."

Sailing down the Rhine after leaving Koblenz, Adelle walked around the track, working off calories from an extra serving of dessert at lunch. She had noticed that her money belt was getting snug.

It's not my fault. The dessert was too good!

The menu had listed dessert as '*Mille-Feuille – vanilla cream Napoleon.*' Adelle had gushed that it was 'to die for.' Her conscience warned her that she would do exactly that – die young like Napoleon if she didn't bring her dessert cravings under control. Nevertheless, Adelle was already looking forward to that night's dinner menu.

"Thanks for inviting me to join your group in Mainz," Jan said as she joined Adelle. "I'm excited about touring the Gutenberg Museum, and Sandy is eager to visit the Opel factory."

"We're happy you're joining us," Adelle replied. She had briefed the girls at lunch, and they were looking forward to meeting Adelle's new friend.

"Did you notice how excited Sandy gets about old cars?" Jan asked. "You should have seen the look on his face in Reims." She sighed. "I wish he would look at me like that."

"That's husbands for you," Adelle said, chuckling. Wes was the same way about his lawnmower.

"This trip has been so timely for Sandy," Jan continued. "He's been stressed at work. I'm glad to see him get away and leave his work behind like he promised."

It seemed to Adelle that everyone back home was experiencing workplace stress. She was grateful that she had retired before her career had consumed all of her time. Now it seemed like people worked 24/7. She thought about Barb. Here they were, sailing along the beautiful Rhine River, and Barb was holed away in her cabin tethered to her laptop. When she joined the girls at mealtime, she seemed very irritable. No matter how hard Adelle tried to include her in upbeat conversations, Barb didn't bite other than to refer to Adelle as "Pollyanna." She was surly and silent, gobbling down her meal and leaving as soon as she was done.

"I liked the program director's comments about Lorelei rock," Jan continued. "Heinrich Heine wrote a famous poem about it in 1824 called 'Die Lorelei.' He describes a siren who sits on the cliff above the Rhine. While combing her golden hair, she distracts shipmen with her beauty and song, causing them to crash into the rocks below."

"Proving that distracted driving isn't a new phenomenon," Adelle said.

"Nor are beautiful women leading men to their death," Jan said. She scanned the deck and lowered her voice. "That's the main reason I'm glad Sandy is away from the office."

For a fleeting moment, Adelle wondered if there were issues between Sandy and Jan that she didn't know about. *Or want to know about.* She didn't know what to say, so she didn't say anything at all. The women walked together in silence.

Adelle turned her thoughts to Barb. She berated herself for being upset with her. After all, Barb didn't have an office anymore. She was out of work and broke. Worse, Teresa had confided that Barb's client had expanded the scope of the investigation, which would mean more work, thus delaying payment. It was "touch and go" whether Barb would be able to make her mortgage payment on time. Still, the Pollyanna name-calling had really started to get to Adelle. What was Barb's problem? Suddenly, Adelle had an idea. Maybe Jan knew why being called Pollyanna had become so negative.

"Jan, do you know the story of Pollyanna?"

Jan stopped walking and faced Adelle, a puzzled look on her face. "Why do you ask?"

"I've never read the book, and I thought maybe you had," Adelle replied.

"I know the book quite well," Jan said, her tone reminding Adelle of a stern teacher. After Adelle explained that her friend kept referring to her derisively as Little Miss Pollyanna, Jan relaxed and smiled.

"Pollyanna was written by Eleanor Porter and was first published in 1913. It's about a cheerful, optimistic girl who always looks on the bright side. No matter what happened to her, she always tried to find at least one good thing about the circumstances."

"It sounds like a good story," Adelle said. "How did being called Pollyanna become a bad thing?"

"To many, she seemed excessively optimistic with no cause. But I think if people knew how her background had affected her, they would see how hard-won her positive attitude was."

Jan explained that Pollyanna was orphaned at the age of eleven. Because of a sense of duty, her maternal aunt had begrudgingly agreed to let Pollyanna live with her.

Before Jan could continue, they were interrupted by Tilly and Debbie. Jan looked at the step counter on her watch, smiled, and said she would see them later.

"Have you seen Barb?" Tilly asked Adelle. "We're learning how to be rude this afternoon. I thought she might be interested."

Rude?

Debbie poked her sister in the ribs and laughed. "Good one." She explained that there would be a presentation in the lounge to teach passengers how to prepare Rudesheim coffee.

"It starts in ten minutes," Tilly said. "If you see Barb, tell her she should join us. We haven't seen her since dinner last night."

"I thought she went shopping with you this morning," Adelle said, remembering the conversation from dinner the previous evening.

"She decided not to," Debbie said.

"Did she say why?" Adelle asked, interested in Barb's excuse.

"She told Teresa to tell us that she didn't like shopping," Tilly replied with a glint in her eye. "As our mother said, honesty is the best policy."

Adelle wished she could get away with blunt honesty. Why did she always feel like she had to make excuses?

"Adelle, are you sure Barb is not working on a case?" Debbie asked.

"Yes," Adelle quickly replied.

Way to go, Adelle. The lies are getting easier all the time.

CHAPTER 5
MAINZ
LOVE A LIE

"What was the name of the guy the Russians mocked?" Tilly asked as she passed the jam for Adelle's toast.

Adelle smiled. She was still feeling like a hero after the previous night's victory. She had provided the right answer to the tie-breaking question: "What was the name of the Koblenz French prefecture mocked by the Russians?" But though she'd known the answer last night, this morning, she couldn't remember. Her smile faded. "James or Jules somebody-or-other?"

"Good memory," Debbie said, chuckling. "Just short."

"Did you see Mr. Grumpy's face when we won?" Tilly asked after the laughter had subsided. "I can't wait to take him on again tonight."

Adelle enjoyed the camaraderie around the breakfast table until Tilly brought up the topic of sailing down the Rhine the previous afternoon.

"I liked the story about love-a-lie rock," Tilly said.

"You mean Lorelei rock," Adelle corrected, stifling a laugh.

"Are you sure it wasn't love-a-lie?" Tilly asked, raising an eyebrow.

Barb snickered, causing Adelle to fume. Barb needed to do her part in this charade. At least she could try to help instead of occasionally gracing them with her presence, wolfing down her boring food with one hand while scrolling through her cellphone with her other hand. She was just plain … Adelle scrambled for the right word. *Rude.* She was just plain rude.

Walking on the tour of Mainz after breakfast, Adelle couldn't shake the feeling that the sisters were beginning to suspect something. It worried her. She didn't want to lose their trust; she enjoyed traveling with the girls too much. She really wanted to go on more trips with them. Adelle knew Debbie and Tilly would never trust her again if they discovered that she had been lying to them. Maybe she should just come clean with the sisters. But then Teresa wouldn't trust her if she broke her promise and told the sisters what was going on. And what about her sense of duty to help Barb? Adelle struggled to pay attention to the guide. *Focus, Adelle, focus.*

Mainz had an interesting story. As their local guide said, walking through Mainz was like walking through two thousand years of history and cultural life.

The oldest part of the city dated back to Roman times. Because of its strategic location on the river, it had acquired considerable economic and political strength. Under Roman rule, it had served as a key northern defense. During the Middle Ages, it was a major trade center.

"Unfortunately," their guide said, "war and destruction are also part of our history. During the second world war, the city was flattened." He pointed out many buildings that had been carefully restored after the war.

Walking along the Rhine promenade, Adelle learned about the friendly rivalry between Mainz and Wiesbaden. Separated by the Rhine River, both cities were capitals of their respective states. As the guide proudly pointed out why Mainz was better, Adelle thought about the good-natured competitiveness between Debbie and Tilly. They were each determined to contribute more to the nightly trivia contest in the lounge. Even Debbie was carrying a notepad now. Adelle wondered what would happen that night. Passengers would be competing in pairs rather than groups. Adelle really hoped Tilly would pick her for a partner. Tilly was the best with details, while Adelle didn't have a chance.

Adelle observed Jan walking ahead with a sister on either side. She could hear Debbie chatting about European fashion trends while Tilly pointed out the historical features and facts that their guide had skipped. The sibling rivalry continued, thought Adelle with a sinking feeling. Jan was obviously the desired trivia partner.

Adelle thought more about the Pollyanna story Jan had continued telling Adelle before the sisters had stolen her away. At the start, Pollyanna's aunt had been mean to her until Pollyanna won her over with the "glad game." Pollyanna's father had taught her the glad game before he died. She had asked for a doll, but when they opened the missionary barrel, all it contained was a child's set of crutches. So he told her to find a way to be glad about them.

"I ask students to imagine asking for a doll from Santa and finding crutches instead," Jan had said.

Adelle couldn't imagine what that had felt like. "Did Pollyanna find a way to be glad?"

Jan's eyes had twinkled. "She decided that she was glad she didn't need them!"

Adelle was impressed. The story reminded her to quit worrying so much and look on the brighter side more often.

Turning the corner, Adelle came face-to-face with the Mainz Cathedral. Teresa was staring up in awe at the soaring red sandstone icon.

"The cathedral is more than a thousand years old," their guide said. "Although builders started the cathedral in 975, most of what you see today was built between the eleventh and thirteenth centuries." He pointed out the cathedral's six magnificent towers and the various architectural differences. Multiple restorations had been required after many destructive fires and wars.

There was a service taking place, so the tour group wasn't able to enter through the large bronze door. "Perhaps you will want to return on your own time later," the guide said before leading them up the highest hill in the town to another church.

"St. Stephen's was originally built on this spot in

990. It was known as the 'Empire's Place of Prayer,'" their guide said. It, too, had been severely damaged in the second world war. The cloister had been rebuilt between 1968 and 1971. The guide directed their attention to the stunning blue stained-glass windows. Adelle was amazed. They were definitely worth the uphill hike to see them.

"In 1973, Marc Chagall was contacted to complete the restoration of St. Stephen's. Nine windows were installed, the first in 1978." The guide smiled. "In 1978, Chagall was ninety-one years old."

Ninety-one?

"Like I always say, age is just a number," Tilly whispered beside her. "It's never too late to contribute."

"Pinch me," Jan murmured. She stood beside Adelle at the Gutenberg Museum as they listened to their knowledgeable host.

"Prior to 1450, when Johannes Gutenberg perfected the printing press to be used commercially, books had to be copied by hand," the museum host said. "Today, we take books for granted, but one hand-copied book in the fourteenth century cost as much as a house."

That fact surprised Adelle.

"In 1300 AD, the largest European library was the university library of Paris, housing three hundred manuscripts. After the development of the printing press, the mass production of books enabled the rapid dissemination of knowledge throughout Europe. In Renaissance Venice, a project to educate only a few wealthiest elites became a project to put a library in every medium-sized town, and a library in the house of every wealthy merchant family."

Adelle thought about the introduction of computers and cellphones in her lifetime. Now everyone had access to a library, literally in the palm of their hand.

"Martin Luther's crusade against the selling of indulgences coincided with an explosion of printing presses across Europe."

"What were indulgences?" Adelle quietly asked Jan.

"Medieval get-out-of-jail-free cards," she replied.

"They were used by the Church to make money," Tilly grumbled. Debbie motioned to her sister to keep her voice down. Tilly ignored her. "You could *pay* to be absolved from sin and to be freed from purgatory after death."

Adelle learned about the ninety-five theses that Luther had nailed to the church door in Wittenberg on October 31, 1517, and the resulting protests demanding reform. It was the first time she connected "Protestant" and "Reformation" to Luther's actions.

It's never too late to learn, Adelle.

Their host held up a reproduction of the theses. "The broadsheet copies of this document were printed in London as quickly as seventeen days later."

Seventeen days was 'quickly'?

"Luther's translation of the New Testament into German sold five thousand copies in just two weeks.

From 1518 to 1525, his writings accounted for a third of all the books sold in Germany," their host said. "His German Bible has gone through more than four hundred and thirty editions."

"The first bestseller," Debbie quipped.

The highlight of the museum was watching the printing press in action. When their guide asked for volunteers to help demonstrate, Debbie thrust her cellphone at Tilly. "Video me," she said before hurrying up to the platform before anyone else could raise their hand. The group watched as Debbie squeezed a screw-type wine press down onto the inked metal type.

Afterward, Debbie accepted the finished printed page from the host and gave it to Tilly. "A souvenir for you, Sis." Tilly thanked Debbie before she handed the page to Jan. "For your school library back home."

Jan placed her hand on her heart.

Tilly smiled. "Like Adelle always says, it's okay to cry. It's just your heart coming out your eyes."

"The printing press was the key to unlocking the modern age," their museum host said, wrapping up the tour. "Inexpensive mass-produced books on every imaginable topic plus revolutionary ideas and priceless ancient knowledge were placed in the hands of every literate European. Knowledge was spread wider and faster than ever before. Civilization never looked back."

"Good try," Debbie said, laughing at Adelle's pitiful attempt to describe the Mainz excursion to Barb at dinner that night. Since Barb had missed the walking tour, simply telling the girls that she had other things to do, Adelle had decided to bring the excursion to her. At first, Adelle had faithfully repeated to Barb what she had learned at the Gutenberg Museum, describing the advancements made possible by the printing press. Barb had seized the opportunity to deliver a long lecture. "That's nothing compared to what technology can do now," Barb had begun. Eventually, Adelle had tuned her out. As she scanned her menu, she laughed to herself when she realized she was experiencing a sudden craving for haricot beans.

After the main course, invigorated by the thought of the desserts to come, Adelle had started to tell Barb about the cathedrals but couldn't keep all the details straight.

"You should have seen them, Barb," Teresa said, launching into a detailed description.

As Adelle tuned Teresa out, she wondered how to entice Tilly to pick her as a partner for the lounge game that night. She was startled when she heard "Earth calling Adelle."

Tilly was grinning at her. "Would you be my partner tonight?"

Pinch me! Adelle was thrilled.

Until Tilly revealed what the program director had told her when they came back from touring Mainz.

"Tonight, we're going to be playing Liar's Club."

64

CHAPTER 6
SPEYER
JUMP

One of Adelle's favorite cruise rituals was preparing a specialty coffee at the coffee station each morning, taking it back to her cabin, and enjoying her first cup of the day while admiring the scenery from her French balcony. She was happy to run into Teresa at the station, juggling a tray with two cups.

"Let me guess," Adelle said. "One-third regular, two-thirds decaf, and lots of hot milk."

"Good memory," Teresa said, laughing. "Who knew getting Barb's morning coffee could be so complicated!"

"No kidding," Adelle said.

Teresa grinned as she poured the coffee. "You and Tilly cleaned up at the Liar's Club contest last night."

Adelle knew she was blushing. She couldn't take any credit; she had simply followed Tilly's lead. Despite Adelle's original fears and doubts, the evening had been a lot of fun. There were three panelists: the maître d', the bartender, and the head chef. In each round, they were given the same obscure word. They were instructed to share the word's history and definition and then use it in an example. Each of them came up with outlandish answers, but only one response was actually correct. The passengers had to guess which answer was true. Tilly was right in every round. She was a walking lie detector.

Teresa looked over the pastry selection. "Breakfast for Barb in our cabin again," she explained.

"Has she finished her work yet?" Adelle asked hopefully as she checked out the chocolate croissants. Perhaps just one wouldn't hurt before breakfast in the ship's restaurant.

"Not quite," Teresa replied. She balanced a blueberry muffin on the wobbly tray. "Barb said she had one more task today. Hopefully, by tomorrow evening, her report will be filed, and her payment will be deposited."

"Good thing you found her some paying work," Adelle said.

"To be honest, this case should help me as well. I hope her client will introduce me to the owner of his company, a large wholesaler." Teresa said, eyes dancing. "This could be a very good connection for our firm."

Although Adelle was pleased that Barb would be paid and that Teresa might benefit as well, she was even more delighted that the case would soon be closed. "Can we share this news with Debbie and Tilly now?" she asked.

"Not quite yet," Teresa said. "Let's wait until Barb gives us the go-ahead."

Soon, Adelle. Soon.

"I'm excited about today," Teresa said as she steadied her tray by rearranging the coffee cups and muffin. "We're going to tour the Speyer Cathedral. It's the top site on my UNESCO bucket list." She set the tray back down and explained why the cathedral was a pivotal structure in European architecture. "It was historically, artistically, and architecturally one of the most significant examples of Romanesque architecture in Europe," Teresa began.

Smile and nod, Adelle. Smile and nod.

"Speyer is over 2000 years old," their local guide said as they started the fifteen-minute walk from the dock into Speyer. He was quite a character, introducing himself as Herman the German. "Thankfully, we were mostly spared from damage during the second world war. The town only lost six of its buildings which was a miracle for this region of Germany." Herman stopped walking and faced the group. "Do you know why we were spared?"

Adelle had no idea.

Herman's eyes twinkled. "Because nothing of importance happened here."

As the walking tour continued, Adelle found herself mulling over what Herman had just said. Nothing of importance had happened in her life since retirement. Sure, it was exciting to be involved with her kids and grandkids, and trips to the lake and golfing filled in her time. But that was the point. She didn't want to go through the rest of her life "filling in time." She wanted to travel, explore, learn, have adventures, to meet people. And she didn't want to do that alone. Wes was her first choice of travel companion, but early in their marriage, they had agreed to pursue activities together that they *both* liked. He liked working with his accounting clients, puttering in their yard, and helping his friend at his farm. He would never use the term "fulfilled," yet he seemed content with his day-to-day life. Adelle needed more. Fortunately, Wes had supported her desire to travel with the girls again. She appreciated his encouragement and support. "The world is your oyster," he had said before kissing her goodbye at the airport. "Have fun and enjoy."

Adelle was having fun, and enjoying being with the girls again. Even Barb, who always added a sense of intrigue and mystery to the trip. Adelle wondered who and what Barb was investigating? She automatically assumed Barb would be successful. She was so passionate about the task at hand. Like Tilly, who was passionate about healthy aging, and Debbie, who was passionate about her store and her customers, and Teresa, who was passionate about her UNESCO bucket list. Something was missing in Adelle's life. She wished she knew what it was.

You miss working with other people.

Yes, that was it! Adelle suddenly realized how much she missed working with other people. Before she retired, she was passionate about working alongside her two younger partners, relishing the challenges, the accomplishments, and the daily high fives when they accomplished their goals.

She missed the excitement, the teamwork, and working with like-minded people with a common purpose. Like when the girls solved mysteries on their last two trips together – that was fun!

Another thought surfaced. Did it bother her that Barb was working on something without her? Perhaps.

You helped a little, Adelle.

Okay, she had helped a little. *By lying.* She had lied to Debbie and Tilly, her friends. Now they didn't trust her. "Are you sure?" they kept asking her. "Are you sure you want another dessert?" "Are you sure Barb isn't coming?" They seemed to be questioning her about everything. She battled with her conscience.

You were just trying to help, Adelle.

I thought white lies wouldn't matter.

They led to more lies.

But I simply wanted to avoid hurting the sisters' feelings.

You should have told them the truth right from the start.

Why do I always start with good intentions, fail, and feel guilty?

Because you're human, Adelle.

From this moment on, I'm going to tell the truth. No matter what.

Good luck with that.

Noticing Sandy talking to Herman, Adelle recalled bumping into Sandy the night before. She had been heading back to her cabin during a break in the liar's game. Sandy sat at the computer station shuffling through papers and frowning at the screen.

"Is there anything I can help you with?" Adelle had asked.

He had quickly flipped the papers over, stood up, and reached into his pocket.

"For your grandson," Sandy said, opening his hand. It contained a red Opel toy car. "Sorry it's not wrapped."

Adelle gratefully accepted the gift. Her grandson would be thrilled.

"I really appreciate you inviting Jan to join your group in Mainz," Sandy had said. "If it wasn't for you, I would have skipped the Opel excursion and gone to the museum. Jan means too much to me to disappoint her. But thanks to you, we both had a wonderful day."

Adelle stumbled on the path when she was startled by a loud complaint behind her. "Are we ever going to get there?" She recognized the voice. It was Mrs. Grumpy. For goodness sakes, Adelle thought. It's only a fifteen-minute stroll.

The walking tour group arrived at the medieval city gate of Speyer, known as the Old Town Gate.

"You are looking at one of the original sixty-eight towers of the old walls and gates that surrounded Speyer," Herman said. "Construction on this particular gate started in 1230, although it has been added to many times over the centuries. At one hundred and eighty feet, it is one of the largest and most architecturally significant gates of the remaining city gates in Germany."

Adelle followed Debbie as she climbed the gate stairs to get a panoramic photo of the city. They looked down onto Maximilian Street, the oldest and most prosperous street in Speyer. The view was spectacular. Adelle noticed a black fedora with a white band and red feather bobbing up and down in the crowd below. The tip thief! Was he one of the passengers in their group? She hurried down the stairs, but the man in the fedora was nowhere in sight.

Resuming their walk, Herman told them some of the histories of the various old buildings along the central street of Speyer's Old Town. Adelle liked the story of The Old Mint, an imposing Baroque structure built in the midst of the pastel-colored houses. "In the twelfth and thirteenth centuries, there was a series of fierce controversies between the bishops and citizens," Herman said. "Then, in 1294, Speyer became a self-ruling Free Imperial City. In doing so, it earned the right to mint and issue its own coins. The original minter's house stood here, facing the old market square." He told them that Speyer was burned down by the French in 1689. "In 1748, the minter's house was replaced by this building. It became known as the Old Mint. Today it's home to a couple of ground-floor shops and the city treasurer office."

Tilly growled. "It makes me so mad."

"The Old Mint?" Adelle asked, confused.

"No. The town treasury office back home." Tilly crossed her arms. "Our park has been sold." Adelle didn't know what to say. She watched silently as Teresa invited Tilly to walk with her for a bit. Further down the street, Tilly stopped. Adelle held her breath until Tilly turned and hugged Teresa.

Adelle smiled to herself. After the girls had laughed at her idea to devalue Tilly's park by throwing empty bottles around it, she had been determined to find a solution. Where there was a will, there had to be a way. She had been inspired by the creative citizens of Bernkastel, who had avoided taxes by building upward. She had texted her idea to Wes, and he had confirmed its viability. So she had approached Teresa to see if her company had a replacement-property and tax-deferral strategy. They did. Her son loved Adelle's idea to purchase Tilly's park for their portfolio. He was delighted to show support for green spaces in urban areas. The acquisition was a win-win for everyone. What really made Adelle smile, though, was Teresa's answer when Adelle had asked her if the park was a good long-term investment. Teresa had laughed. "As Tilly likes to remind us, life isn't always about money."

At the end of the pedestrian street, the tour group arrived at the Speyer Cathedral. It was enormous. Herman told them it was as long as their cruise ship. Tilly was cheerful again, whistling as she wrote down notes.

"The construction of the red sandstone church began under the reign of Conrad II in the year 1013," Herman said. "It was the most ambitious project of that era. King Conrad was determined to build the western world's largest church. It was supposed to be his resting place. Although neither he nor his son saw the cathedral completed in their lifetime, eight other emperors were buried beneath the church. Now it's a symbol of the former era of imperial power."

Adelle marveled at how long it took to complete construction projects in years past. The builders had to possess infinite patience, knowing that they would never see the final outcome of their efforts. They had to trust that their hopes and dreams would come true.

"Over centuries, the cathedral was enlarged, reconstructed, and altered," Herman said proudly. "Despite several occupations and wars, our cathedral has maintained the overall look of its eleventh-century Romanesque appearance. The vaulted nave and the two sets of towers at each end of the building have set the standard for the construction of churches all over the Rhineland region."

The walking tour concluded with a visit to Judenhof, the central district of the medieval Jewish Quarter in Speyer. Herman told them that the Jewish community had existed in Speyer for more than a thousand years. Then, he led them down the steep and narrow stone steps to the ritual immersion bath, built around 1120.

Back at street level, while Herman was answering questions, Adelle noticed that two people were missing.

Wes was always teasing her about her lifetime habit of counting people whenever she was in a group. He called it her oldest child superpower.

Retracing her steps in search of the missing group members, Adelle found Mr. Grumpy hunched over Mrs. Grumpy, who was sitting on the top stone step to the bath.

"Are you okay?" Adelle asked.

They looked up. It was the first time Adelle had seen Mrs. Grumpy smile. She was a lot younger than Adelle had believed.

"We're fine, thanks. I'm just a little winded after all those steep steps."

After introductions, Adelle chitchatted with the older couple, allowing Gertrude to rest a little longer before rejoining the group. She was surprised how pleasant they were, unlike the intense competitors they had been during the nightly lounge contests. She learned that George and Gertrude were on their first cruise.

"Our children surprised us with this trip," George said.

"To be honest, we were a little put-out and unhappy at the start," Gertrude said. "I have been recovering from a nasty cold and severe jet lag." She turned to George. "My ears finally popped!"

"Great," George said. "No more yelling."

After helping Gertrude to her feet, George picked up his jacket and put his hat on. A black fedora with a white band and red feather.

"You're the tip thief!" Adelle blurted out before covering her mouth with her hand.

George laughed as he turned to his wife. "I told you she saw me at the café in Trier."

Adelle was shocked. First, he was a thief, and now he was laughing and bragging about it.

"Let me explain," George said. "Because of the short notice, I wasn't able to get the right currency before we left for our cruise. And I wanted to tip our local guide, so I picked up the change and added the amount to our bill when I paid with my credit card."

"The kids might regret introducing us to cruising," Gertrude said. "We're already looking at more trips like this."

George chuckled. "We've been joking about what our children would think if we revised our will to read: 'Being of sound mind, we spent it all.'"

Good one, thought Adelle.

"Seriously, we're grateful for every moment of this trip," George said. "We're learning something new every day."

"Especially gratitude," Gertrude added. "I started out unhappy, but I've learned that you can't be grateful and unhappy at the same time."

So true.

Barb was full of surprises when she joined the girls for lunch. She looked radiant. Rather than sporting her usual ponytail, her wavy blonde hair fell in soft waves on her shoulders. Instead of jeans and an old sweatshirt, she was dressed in black slacks and a pale blue sweater. And she was smiling.

Smiling!

"What does everyone recommend for lunch?" Barb asked, scanning the menu, phone nowhere in sight.

What? No hamburgers or hot dogs off the Classics menu?

Adelle couldn't believe that Barb had ordered the same lunch every day. She was in Europe! Time to enjoy the regional cuisine.

While Adelle salivated over the mouthwatering dessert choices, Tilly suggested that Barb start with the orange and carrot soup, followed by the chef's *salade niçoise*. Debbie recommended the *chicken tikka masala*, served with jasmine rice.

Barb finally agreed with Teresa's suggestion and ordered the barbequed pulled-pork sandwich. Adelle ordered the sandwich as well. That would allow room for the peach melba; peaches served with vanilla ice cream, peach syrup, and raspberry sauce. And a small serving of the chocolate mousse.

Once everyone had ordered their lunch, Barb had another surprise in store. She suggested that they visit the Speyer Technik Museum together during their afternoon free time. Adelle was thrilled. At last, all the girls would do something together like one big, happy family.

According to the museum brochure, there were over seventy airplanes displayed inside and outside the numerous halls. As Adelle entered the main hall, she tipped back to admire the diverse airplanes hanging from the roof. Below them, she saw a row of red antique fire trucks. Sandy and George stood next to them, admiring a classic yellow Rolls Royce with green fenders next to a polished apple-red Mercedes.

Adelle blinked. Was that Barb off to the side? Videoing the old cars? *Who knew Barb was an antique car buff!* The day was full of surprises.

After touring the hangar, Adelle went outside to explore more exhibits. She saw Barb and Teresa at the top of a long staircase attached to a jumbo jet. The way the airplane was positioned on its giant stilts, it looked like it was getting ready to land. Heading to the stairway, she noticed a long tube twisting its way from the jet down to the tarmac. She heard a piercing scream before a young girl shot out from the bottom of the tube, grinning from ear to ear. It was a slide!

As Adelle climbed the stairs, she thought about Barb's transformation. It was great to see her in a good mood and smiling again. Perhaps it was finally the right time to ask Barb what she was working on.

The interior of the Boeing 747 was more spacious than Adelle had imagined. It had been partially dismantled to make room for several interactive screens. Some sections were laid out as they would have been when the plane was in service. The cockpit with all its instruments was mindboggling. So many buttons and switches!

Adelle took a deep breath before she went outside to walk between the railings on one of the aircraft wings. She would have to tell Debbie about the great photo opportunity.

Re-entering the jet, Adelle saw Barb and Teresa ahead of her.

"Did you get the video evidence for the motive?" Adelle overheard Teresa ask.

Evidence? Motive?

Curious, Adelle stopped to listen.

"Affirmative," Barb replied.

"Good," Teresa said. "When will you file your final report?"

"Late tomorrow afternoon, just in time to make my mortgage payment."

Good.

Barb chuckled. "Who gets to tell Little Miss Pollyanna that her new friend is stealing to buy antique cars?"

What?!!!

Desperate to get away before they saw her, Adelle frantically searched for an escape. She spotted the entrance to the slide.

Jump, Adelle! Jump!

Adelle couldn't believe George was a thief. There must be a reasonable explanation. Walking back to the ship, she reviewed what she knew about her new friend.

On the one hand, George had demonstrated integrity. Yes, he took the waiter's tip, but he reimbursed the waiter by adding the amount to his bill. Was he telling the truth?

On the other hand, George liked antique cars. He had talked fondly about the antique cars in Reims and the vintage display at the Opel factory. Was he stealing to buy antique cars?

Or to pay for more trips?

No, Adelle decided. George couldn't be a thief. He and Gertrude were so nice.

Too nice?

Adelle kept replaying her previous conversations with Barb, who had lectured the girls about crime. It always involved means, opportunity, and motive.

George didn't need money. He had just sold his business. Gertrude said it would take a thousand world cruises to spend it all.

Were they lying?

Some people love to lie.

Including you, her conscience reminded her.

Adelle needed more information. She decided to join George and Gertrude's trivia team that night.

CHAPTER 7
STRASBOURG
CARPE DIEM

At ten the next morning, Adelle joined Barb, Teresa, Debbie, and Tilly at the ramp just as their local guide introduced herself. Camille explained that the six of them would spend the rest of the morning and afternoon walking through various districts of Strasbourg, shopping for local Alsatian specialties along the way.

"Did you hear that, Adelle?" Debbie asked, eyes dancing as they fell in behind Camille. "We're all going shopping together."

"For food," Adelle said, rolling her eyes. Her stomach rumbled. Because she had tossed and turned all night, she had slept through her alarm and missed breakfast. Her first priority was to find something to eat. Her second priority was to gather more information about Barb's allegation concerning George. After spending the previous evening with George and his wife, she was convinced that he was not a thief. Competitive, yes. A criminal, no.

"Strasbourg is home to a number of important European institutions, including the Council of Europe," Camille said proudly. "The European Parliament hosts sessions here as well as in Brussels."

Adelle inhaled deeply as Camille continued. Was that fresh-baked bread she could smell?

"Strasbourg is also famous for its beautiful historic center – the Grand Ile – which was the first entire city center to be classified as a UNESCO World Heritage site."

Teresa paid rapt attention as Camille pointed out some of the architectural features of the neighborhood. The quaint buildings were ornately decorated, many with high-pitched roofs and multi-dormered windows.

Adelle fell behind the group, hopeful that they couldn't hear her empty stomach complaining.

"Anyone hungry?" Camille asked, stopping in front of a cheese store.

Barb elbowed her way into the shop first, followed closely by Adelle.

The women sampled three kinds of cheese, including a strong-smelling soft cheese with a surprisingly subtle taste. "It's called Munster cheese," Camille said. "It's named after the little town of Munster. Abbeys and monasteries have made this cheese since the Middle Ages."

Adelle chuckled to herself. It was during her own middle age that she had discovered cheese varieties other than cheddar.

As they continued their walk, Debbie teased Adelle

about missing breakfast. "You were probably afraid to join us after Tilly called you a traitor last night."

Adelle couldn't help wincing. She needed to earn George's trust, so she had tried extra hard to help his team do well. She lucked out when the last questions were about the Old Mint. Because of her background in finance, she had been interested in Herman's comments and had easily recalled the historical facts. As a result, they won the trivia contest.

"Is Tilly over her disappointment?" Adelle asked.

"Our father always reminded us to win the things that count." Debbie grinned. "Tonight is the last contest, with a prize for the winner. Tilly is determined to be victorious."

At their next stop, the group sampled from charcuterie plates artfully arranged with special regional sausages, meats, and pickles.

"Save some room for later," Camille said. "We're going to pick up food along the way to take to a winstub."

"A wine tub?" Tilly asked Camille before swallowing the last pickle.

"A winstub," Camille replied. "Winstubs are the Alsatian version of the neighborhood pub. A professional sommelier will teach us the art of pairing local foods with Alsatian and French wines."

"I like him already," Tilly said, winking at Adelle.

Adelle couldn't contain her grin. She was in Tilly's good graces again.

Now that she had some food in her tummy, Adelle

turned her attention to finding the right time and place to talk to Barb privately. The upcoming winstub sounded perfect.

In the meantime, Adelle couldn't help indulging her sweet tooth at the next stop, a bakery full of delicious smelling baguettes and pastries. The shop owner greeted them at the door with a tray of six ring-shaped cakes, called *kugelhopf*, topped with almonds and frosting.

"One story says *kugelhopf* originated in Vienna," Camille said, passing the tray around. "When the Hapsburg forces defeated the Turks at the city gates, the Viennese bakers celebrated by creating cakes in the shape of a sultan's turban."

Adelle took a bite. The *kugelhopf* was light and fluffy, with raisins complementing the bready flavor. She devoured it on the spot.

Entering the bakery, Adelle's mouth watered as she gawked at all the pastries starting with the towers of pastel-colored macarons in front of the case displaying rows of chocolate éclairs.

"You've got frosting on your nose," Debbie said, laughing as she took Adelle's picture.

The raspberry macarons were delicious. "I like how these are crunchy on the outside and gooey on the inside," Adelle said, reaching to sample another one.

"Like Tilly when she doesn't get enough sleep," Debbie said, playfully elbowing her sister.

Sampling the locally popular coconut macarons, Adelle thought of Wes. He loved coconut as much as she loved chocolate. She snuck another éclair sample before Camille saw her.

Who knew shopping could be so much fun!

The winstub felt very cozy, featuring checkered tablecloths and a wood-burning stove. Their charming sommelier paired Alsace Pinot Noir, Riesling, and *Gewürztraminer* with their food purchases. He kept teasing Tilly, challenging her to say *Gewürztraminer* five times in a row. Debbie rolled her eyes as she videoed the animated exchange.

Adelle noticed Barb in the corner, speaking quietly on her cellphone.

Here's your chance, Adelle.

As Adelle walked over, Barb put her phone away. "I was dictating a note to share with my mother. She loves to host wine-pairing parties." Barb seemed radiant as she talked about her mother. Adelle decided business could wait. It was nice to chitchat like old times.

After lunch at the winstub, Camille led the women over a bridge into Petite France, the name given to the medieval city between the rivers. They walked alongside picturesque canals and half-timbered townhouses, leaning out over the narrow cobblestone streets.

"This is La Place Gutenberg," Camille announced. They were surrounded by Renaissance buildings and a lofty gothic cathedral. She pointed to a large statue across the square. "That is a statue of Johannes Gutenberg, the inventor of the modern-day printing press." Adelle noticed Sandy taking a picture of Jan smiling in front of the statue. They seemed like such a happy couple.

Adelle was distracted by music from the carousel on the corner. Children laughed as they rode the swirling horses and mermaids glittering in the afternoon sun. The scene reminded her of Lorelei rock. *Love-a-lie, love-a-lie* kept going around and around in her head. With a start, she remembered Barb's accusation. She needed to find out the truth, clear George, and apologize to Tilly and Debbie for lying to them the past few days.

After strolling around Petite France, Camille finally led them to another cozy winstub where the resident chef taught them how to make *flammkuchen*. To Barb's visible relief, he described it as a German pizza without tomatoes. The base was thin and crispy, topped with a blend of cream, cheese, local ham, and onions. While it was cooking, the women enjoyed mingling with the other patrons and sampling beer from the local brewery.

When it was time to sit down and eat, Adelle planned to sit beside Barb, but she was missing.

"She's gone back to the ship," Teresa said.

"Before the pizza was ready?" Adelle asked. Barb had been excited to eat "real food."

"She had to get back for the final call with her client," Teresa replied quietly.

Adelle's legs went rubbery. She had missed her opportunity, and now it was too late. Barb was about to make a huge mistake. Thinking quickly, she asked their server for a takeout container. "I have to get back there myself," Adelle said.

"What should I say if the sisters ask about you?" Teresa asked.

"You'll think of something," Adelle replied before rushing out the door.

Adelle stood in front of Barb's cabin door, debating whether she should get involved. What if Barb got angry and never talked to her again? What if Adelle was alienated forever from Barb and the rest of the girls?

Adelle, when did you start worrying about the worst that could happen instead of the best-case scenario?

The worst that can happen is if an innocent man is wrongly accused.

And the best-case scenario?

I prevent Barb from making a horrible mistake.

Carpe diem, Adelle.

Adelle squared her shoulders and knocked on the cabin door. "Pizza delivery," she said loudly.

Barb opened the door, and Adelle barged in.

Just then, the timer on Barb's cellphone rang.

"You have to leave," Barb sputtered. "I have an important call to attend to."

Adelle stood her ground. "I'm not leaving. You are about to make a big mistake."

Barb glared at Adelle. "I haven't got time for this."

She hurriedly sat down at the small table and opened her laptop. "Hide."

Adelle dove under the table.

"I've got the video you requested," Adelle heard Barb say.

"Show it to me," a deep voice demanded.

As Barb walked over to the bed to get her cell-phone, Adelle's left calf cramped. Without thinking, she popped out from under the table and found herself face to face with a bald man glaring at her from the laptop screen. Intimidated by his fierce stare, Adelle dropped her eyes to the nameplate on his desk. The company name seemed familiar. Where had she seen it before?

"Who are you?" the man demanded.

Breathe, Adelle.

"I'm Barb's mother," Adelle said, forcing a smile. *Where did that come from?* "I came to get my book."

Barb turned the screen so that Adelle was out of view. "Time to leave, Mother," she said through clenched teeth.

Adelle blurted out the first thing that came into her brain. "Enjoy your therapy session, Barb. I'll see you on the deck later."

Adelle stomped her way to the door, opened it, paused, then shut it loudly. She turned back to Barb and put her finger up to her lips.

"Sorry about that," Barb said, speaking to the screen. "My mother is such a pain. She talked her way onto my cruise at the last minute."

"What about the therapy comment?" Adelle heard the man ask.

"She barged in here to get her book. I told her to be quick as my ex-employer had offered outplacement counseling via this conference call. Now she thinks I'm in therapy."

Adelle held her breath. Would Barb's client fall for it? And when did Barb turn into such a good liar?

Hello, Pot.

"I've collated the altered documents." Barb held her cellphone up to the screen. "And I've got the antique car video evidence."

"Good work. As soon as you forward the video and your report, I'll deposit your fee."

"How do I know I can trust you?" Barb asked.

"Ask your therapist," the man said.

Barb closed her laptop. The call was over.

Adelle got right to the point. "George is not a thief."

Barb stared at her. "Affirmative," she finally said.

"Then why were you videoing George standing in front of the antique cars?" Adelle asked.

"I wasn't videoing George."

Adelle replayed the scene in her mind. She had walked into the hangar, looked at the airplanes hanging from the ceiling, and then saw George and Sandy looking at the antique cars. Her stomach clenched. George was standing beside Sandy.

George was standing beside Sandy!

Adelle recalled what the nameplate said: Pipedream Division Manager.

Sandy worked for Pipedream. Wait a minute! Was *Sandy* the thief?

Adelle searched her memory bank, reviewing her interactions with Sandy and Jan. Jan lied to Sandy about counting steps. Was Sandy lying to Jan, too? About not working while on vacation? Adelle remembered him frowning at the ship's computer screen as he shuffled through a stack of papers. What was he doing? Stealing from his employer to buy antique cars? Or was something else going on?

With a sinking feeling, Adelle remembered Jan's comment about the siren of Lorelei rock. Was Sandy living a double life? Living a lie?

Adelle shook her head. No, he adored Jan.

"If George is not the thief, then who is?" Adelle asked, dreading the answer.

"Sandy."

"No! He can't be!"

Breathe, Adelle, breathe. "What are the facts?" she demanded.

Step by step, Barb presented the evidence. She had remotely combed through the financial statements to trace the diverted funds. Sandy had stolen from his employer. "He had access to the accounts, providing the means and the opportunity," Barb said, summing up her investigation.

Adelle had to admit that the case sounded straightforward.

"What about the motive?" Adelle asked.

"Antique cars. He needed money to support his car obsession."

"Is that fact or opinion?"

Barb twirled her hair. "Deduction."

Adelle's spider senses started to tingle. Something didn't add up.

Was it a coincidence that Sandy was on this cruise at the same time as Barb? A cruise that Sandy's boss had arranged for him?

Barb's client contacted Teresa, who arranged the call with Barb after the trip began.

When Teresa had met Sandy's manager at the conference, had she mentioned that she and Barb were planning to be on this very cruise?

Possibly. The client was Sandy's boss. He hired Barb.

But Sandy said his boss detested consultants.

Then why did he hire Barb?

Adelle took a deep breath. "Barb, is it possible that you're wrong?"

Barb's eyes narrowed. "The facts point to Sandy. There are no anomalies in the data I've examined." Barb started to present the evidence again.

"Stop," Adelle commanded. "Is it possible that someone else had access to the data? Someone who knew that Sandy was locked out of the accounts?"

Barb stood silently and stared at her laptop. She raised her head and looked Adelle in the eye.

"We need to talk to Sandy."

Adelle was impressed with Barb's interrogation skills. With collaborating information from Sandy, Barb and Adelle had put the pieces of the puzzle together. Sandy had lied to Jan – he had brought work with him on their trip. "Adelle, please don't tell Jan about this," he had pleaded. "What she doesn't know won't hurt her." He had shown Barb the dated reports he had printed before leaving for the river cruise. The reports were different than the reports Barb had reviewed.

Barb shared what had happened. On her first conference call, Sandy's boss had instructed her to change the department's passwords, a standard practice whenever questions arose. Sandy was locked out of the accounts. His boss was then free to redirect funds, making it appear as if Sandy was stealing from the company. The diverted funds equaled the price of the cruise plus one hundred thousand dollars. His boss would deny that he had arranged Sandy's trip as a company gift. Sandy would be blamed for the theft.

The means and the opportunity were evident, but what was the motive? Remembering that Jan had told her Sandy was stressed about something at his office, Adelle had questioned him about it. Sandy confirmed that his new manager was having an affair with one of the women in the department. With Sandy discredited, his boss would promote his girlfriend to take over Sandy's job. He also confirmed that everyone knew about his passion for antique cars. His boss had correctly assumed that Sandy would tour the vintage car display at the Technik Museum in Speyer, providing an opportunity for Barb to video the alleged motive.

After questioning Sandy, Barb had arranged a call with the owner of the large wholesale conglomerate that had recently bought Pipedream. As she presented her case, the owner had listened carefully, asking for clarification when needed. He had promised to contact Barb as soon as he had investigated the allegations himself.

"Good work helping Barb with her investigation," Teresa said, sitting beside Adelle as they waited for the nightly lounge contest to begin. "Barb filled me in."

"I hope our assumptions are correct," Adelle said. "But I'm concerned about Barb. Now she won't be paid, and she'll miss her mortgage payment."

"Regardless, you did the right thing," Teresa said. "Neither Barb nor I want to benefit from an innocent person being framed for a crime he didn't commit."

Adelle remembered that Teresa had something at stake as well. "Sorry, I forgot Barb's client had made networking promises to you after you introduced him to Barb."

Teresa's face reddened. "He used me. He was a liar."

Adelle looked down at her lap. "So am I." She told Teresa about all the times she had lied to Debbie and Tilly. She was ashamed of herself.

"They'll understand," Teresa said as the contest was about to begin. "You worry too much."

Easy for you to say, Adelle thought. Everyone trusts you.

The theme of the trivia game that night was "name that tune." Passengers were invited to write down requests, including the name of the song title and the artist. The pianist played short sound bites, then the other passengers wrote down their guesses. George's group accumulated the most points until Tilly suggested that extra points be awarded for dancing. She handed her request to the piano player. Grinning, he played a lively polka. Tilly grabbed Barb, and they danced together around the small dance area.

Barb submitted a request for the next song. When the piano player shrugged his shoulders and shook his head, Barb set her cellphone up in front of his microphone. Adelle got points for recognizing one of her grandchildren's favorite songs. Debbie giggled as she videoed Tilly collecting more points and imitating Barb's wild gyrations.

Adelle had an idea. The piano player grinned as he played her request, the popular children's folk song about dancing on the bridge at Avignon. The girls danced together while the program director videoed the five of them on Debbie's phone. Afterward, the program director declared that with bonus points awarded for dancing, their group had easily won first prize. To Debbie's delight, it was a discount coupon for shopping in the ship's small store. Then, to Adelle's delight,

George gallantly surprised them with a bottle of Reims champagne.

In all the merriment, Adelle had forgotten about the anticipated call from the owner of Sandy's company until it was time to say goodnight.

"Meet me at the coffee station before breakfast," Barb said. "I'm sure to hear from him before morning."

CHAPTER 8
BASEL
A GOOD TEAM

After breakfast, Adelle and her friends bade a fond farewell to the ship's crew before they disembarked to start the final two days of their trip in Basel and Zurich. The mystery that had begun on the Moselle River had been solved on the Rhine. The owner had confirmed their suspicions. Now Adelle was looking forward to the right time to come clean with the sisters. She really wanted to cruise with them again and hoped they would forgive her.

Teresa joined Adelle as they started their walking tour through the cluster of medieval buildings spread out on the hilly riverbank of Basel.

"Thanks again for worrying about George and Sandy," Teresa said.

"I thought you told me not to worry so much," Adelle replied, trying not to smirk.

"Barb told me that if you hadn't intervened, she would have made a terrible mistake."

Adelle recalled her meeting with Barb at the coffee station that morning. Pipedream's owner had called during the night. The missing funds had been recovered, and Sandy's boss had been fired. He had not been reimbursed for the cost of Sandy and Jan's trip. Served him right, Adelle had thought. Even better, the owner had paid Barb generously, enabling her to more than make her mortgage payment on time.

On top of that, he had organized a meeting between Barb and a connection he had with his insurance company whose headquarters were in Zurich. "With the head of their investigation department," Barb had said. Thanks to Barb's suggestion, he had also arranged for Teresa to meet with their Zurich sales department. With any luck, Teresa would secure lower corporate insurance premiums.

Adelle was pleased that everything had turned out so well for her friends, but she was disappointed that they were leaving the trip early. The insurance company was sending a limo to pick them up for meetings after lunch, with additional appointments scheduled for the following day.

As they walked behind their local tour guide, Teresa shared that Barb's biggest career concern was job security.

"I told her that in my opinion, the best job security is to work for yourself," Teresa said. She was confident Barb possessed the skills to work on contract as an independent investigator.

"She's very talented," Teresa continued. "Once her

reputation is firmly established, she will have no trouble building her business through referrals."

The group stopped in front of an animated sculpture fountain.

"This fountain was created by Jean Tinguely in 1977," the local guide said. "This is where the stage of the old city theater company once stood. The artist lined this shallow fountain with black asphalt and created these mechanical figures. As you can see, they're in constant motion and conversation with each other, much like the mime artists, actors, and dancers who used to perform here."

"This fountain reminds me of you and Barb," Teresa said, turning to Adelle.

"It does?"

"Yes," Teresa said, smiling. "As I told Barb, your personalities are very different, but you have complementary skills. She's naturally skeptical while you focus on the positives. She's good with technology, and you're good with people."

Adelle silently agreed that she and Barb were very different. While Barb always questioned people's ulterior motives, Adelle always assumed they were good. Her family was always teasing her about being so naïve.

"When you communicate, you work well together," Teresa said. "You respect each other's abilities and experiences, and you both have a strong sense of right and wrong. You make a good team."

A good team. Adelle liked what Teresa was saying.

Their local guide stopped in front of Basel's

Münster Cathedral. It was very distinctive, with red sandstone walls and bright, colorful roof tiles.

Inside, they walked over a glass panel protecting a stone with a mythical creature etched on it. It looked like a combination of a dragon and a rooster.

"It's called a basilisk," their guide said. "The locals believe that if you make a wish while standing on the stone, your wish will come true, and you will have good luck."

The girls took turns standing on the stone while Debbie took their picture. When it came to Adelle's turn, she crossed her fingers as she made her own private wish.

Their last stop was the Basel town hall.

"Another rat house," Debbie said, giggling.

Their guide suggested they sign the Rathaus guest book. "Write down what you desire, and supposedly it will come true." Adelle made sure she was the last one in their group to write down her wish and sign the book. She was pleased to see Barb waiting for her outside.

"So, Little Miss Pollyanna, what did you wish for?"

The old Adelle would have bristled with indignation. But the new Adelle had learned to be more direct with Barb. "Why do you call me that?" she asked.

"Because you are always so *happy, happy*," Barb replied. "You can really be annoying sometimes."

Hello, Pot.

It was time to have a heart-to-heart with Barb. As they talked, she discovered that Barb hadn't answered her chatty emails before the trip because she was worried about losing her job.

"That doesn't mean I wasn't looking forward to seeing you," Barb said, digging through her day pack. "Here, I got something for you in Reims." She handed Adelle a small wrapped package. It was a Christmas ornament - the smiling angel of Reims. Adelle studied the ornament and tried not to cry. The angel looked so …

Tranquil.

"Why didn't you tell me what was going on?" Adelle asked, realizing how much Barb's secrecy had bothered her. "Don't you trust me?"

"I trust you, but I thought you weren't interested."

What?

"Why?"

"We were standing in the courtyard at the Porta Nigra in Trier," Barb said in a small voice, "when I started to tell you about the corporate raiders who had cost me my job, but you rushed away."

Adelle was shocked. She thought about all the consequences of that one misunderstanding. If only she had been more direct with Barb right from the start.

It's not too late, Adelle.

One by one, Adelle shared the reasoning behind her decisions and actions. Pretty soon, both she and Barb were laughing at the absurdity of it all.

"I think we've both learned a lesson," Barb said, wiping tears of laughter away. "We need to communicate better."

So true.

Barb pointed out Jan and Sandy, walking hand in hand ahead of them. "Sandy might be promoted," Barb commented. "His employer has a renewed appreciation for company loyalty."

Adelle noticed Sandy's attention momentarily diverted by an antique car driving by. As he turned his head, Jan took a quick peek at her watch. Adelle smiled. Each couple had their own patterns, she realized, as she and Barb strolled along in companionable silence. Traveling was healthy for relationships. Getting away put things into perspective. She had forgotten about her renovation woes until breakfast that morning. When she had mentioned her hopes for her kitchen cabinets, Tilly had been adamant that the oak be preserved as it was. She insisted that Adelle and Wes were creating a heritage home. Debbie had suggested painting the walls instead of the oak cabinets. Teresa had agreed. "Leave the cabinets as they are," she had advised. "Oak cabinets are making a comeback." They had all laughed when Debbie had turned to her sister. "A comeback? There's hope for your cargo pants yet!"

Thinking about the cabinets again, Adelle realized that she and Wes could do a better job of communicating as well. She was confident that they could find a solution that would work for both of them.

After the walking tour, the women had lunch together before the insurance company limo arrived.

"Before we leave, I have some explaining to do," Barb said, passing around a plate of ham and cheese croquettes. She told Debbie and Tilly that she had been working on a confidential case that she was not at liberty to share.

"Adelle covered for me," Barb said.

"Did you lie to us, Adelle?" Debbie asked, eyes twinkling.

Uh-oh…

Think, Adelle. You're still not at liberty to tell the truth, the whole truth, and nothing but the truth.

"I never lie," Adelle finally said, smiling sweetly. "And that's the truth."

Barb laughed the loudest, rolling her eyes like Debbie always did.

"Teresa and I are meeting with an international insurance company in Zurich this afternoon and then again tomorrow," Barb said after the laughter had subsided.

"This is goodbye?" Tilly asked.

"Affirmative." Barb smiled. "Until we meet again in Portugal."

Adelle's first wish had come true. When they had sat down to lunch, Tilly had ordered a round of port. Debbie then shared that she had talked to some other passengers who had raved about their Portugal river cruise.

"Adelle, will you host us on the cruise of the Duoro River in Portugal?" Tilly had asked.

Adelle was thrilled. Everyone agreed to go cruising together again.

Tilly took another croquette as she started to brief Barb and Teresa on what they would miss on the Zurich city walk and the scenic boat tour of the lake. "Zurich's Old Town is home to many colorful guild houses and several historic churches," she began.

Debbie interrupted. "We need to eat up. There's shopping to do. Sis and I saw the cutest chocolate molds of the Basel Town Hall and Munster Cathedral. We're buying some for our grandchildren." She turned to Teresa. "They are architectural masterpieces. Your son will love them!"

Adelle and Barb declined the invitation to shop and ordered coffee instead.

"I have something to show you," Barb said, passing her cellphone to Adelle after the others rushed away. "I've been designing a new business card."

Adelle's hands started to tingle as she read the card. She looked up at Barb. "It states your name, followed by 'and Associates.'"

Barb grinned. "Times have changed," she said. "It's easy to work remotely now. On a ship. With trusted friends. And cleaning service, meals, and morning coffee." She grinned at Adelle. "Served just the way I like it."

Adelle sighed contentedly. Her second wish had

come true. She was already looking forward to more mysteries to solve.

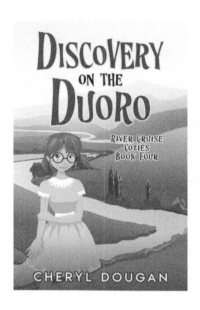

Hop Aboard *Discovery on the Duoro: River Cruise Cozies Book Four!*

She expected to relax on her river cruise through Portugal. She didn't expect threats from the mafia. Will Adelle discover the missing port before her new career sinks?

Read a sample of the first chapter of the next book for free!
Enter this address to get it delivered to your email!
https://tinyurl.com/cheryldougan4

GOOD KARMA

Thank you for reading *Mystery on the Moselle!*

Please take a moment to review this book. Your honest review will help future readers decide if they want to take a chance on a new-to-them author! An honest review is the greatest gift you can give an author.

You can go to the book directly on Amazon and leave a review!

If interested, please follow my author page on Amazon to learn about new releases! https://www.amazon.com/author/cheryldougan

ALSO BY CHERYL DOUGAN

RIVER CRUISE COZIES

A River Cruise Travel Mystery Series

Available on Amazon and Kindle Unlimited

She gladly came out of retirement. She never expected to be cruising down the Danube trying to catch a diamond thief red-handed.

If you like globe-trotting heroines, quirky casts, and spectacular settings, then you'll love Cheryl Dougan's glittering whodunit.

She is excited to river cruise with her girlfriends again. But when one of them goes missing, can she solve the mystery before life goes overboard?

Will Adelle unravel all the mysteries in time to rescue her friends and regain their trust?

If you like armchair travel and heartwarming stories of friendship, you'll love Cheryl Dougan's sparkling new tale of intrigue.

Adelle is excited to get away on another river cruise with her girlfriends. But when her old friends accuse her new friends of theft, can she navigate the truth before all their careers sink?

Can Adelle solve the mystery and save everyone's reputation from sinking?

If you like unique characters, disentangling mysteries, and armchair travel in European settings, then you'll love Cheryl Dougan's newest tale of navigating friendships and intrigue.

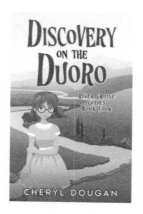

She expected to relax on her river cruise through Portugal. She didn't expect threats from the mafia.

Will Adelle discover the missing port before her new career sinks?

ABOUT THE AUTHOR

Cheryl has always loved reading and travelling. Recently she discovered her passion for writing travel cozy mysteries. When she is not reading, writing, or planning her next trip, she enjoys being outdoors, listening to her characters as they get excited about their next escapade.

Cheryl is the author of *Diamonds on the Danube*, *Passageways and Provence*, *Mystery on the Moselle*, and *Discovery on the Duoro*.

While she makes her home in Saskatchewan, Canada she is always on the lookout for her next adventure!

Find Cheryl online at: **www.cheryldouganauthor.com**

Made in United States
North Haven, CT
14 October 2022

25446498R00075